In one swift pounce Tallulah Mimosa is balancing on my windowsill. The fluttering of pigeons sounds like angel wings.

"I'm looking for Sue Slate, Private Eye," she says, her voice like a juicy purr.

"At your service," I reply with a suave tone I keep handy for just such emergencies. Bowing, I am meanwhile disengaging from my former pounce stance in as graceful a manner as I can muster. I gesture to a clear patch of shelving for her to sit on.

And sit she does, like this is what she came for. Like she is paid to do it for a living. Like this is the greatest performance of her lives. I am spellbound as she lowers herself with a slinky sinuous move she does not learn at any Catlick school. She smooths her multi-colored jumpsuit — black, gold, cream — with a manicured paw. The left side of her face is solid black, a half-mask which dips down her nose like a roller coaster giving a thrill. It splashes across her delicate upper lip, her right cheek, and ends somewhere under the jumpsuit. Right at her neck, like an oversized piece of fourteen carat ice, is a flash of blinding white fur. She wears Roemance, the ritzy scent sold exclusively at Cats Fifth Avenue.

SUE SLATE

PRIVATE EYE
by Lee Lynch

The Naiad Press, Inc.
1989

Printed in the United States of America
First Edition

Edited by Christine Cassidy
Cover design by Pat Tong and Bonnie Liss
    (Phoenix Graphics)
Typeset by Sandi Stancil

Library of Congress Cataloging-in-Publication Data

Lynch, Lee, 1945—
    Sue Slate : private eye.

    I. Title.
PS3562.Y426S8 1989   813'.54   89-12653
ISBN 0-941483-52-5

This book is dedicated to:

Sue
Thomas
Sweetpea
Canterbury Tailes
Ragbag
Mercedes
(and to the late)
Edison Weagle
Gordie Feiden
Beckett
Sojourner
Richard
Maxwell Perkins
Mergatroyd

I wish to thank for their encouragement in this madcap literary adventure: Carol Seajay, Hawk Madrone, Tee Corinne, Christi Cassidy, Bernie Gardner and, to my delight, Akia Woods.

A percentage of the royalties from this book will be divided between a local chapter of the Humane Society, and The Ruby House Foundation, P.O. Box 182, Dillard, Oregon 97432, which provides care for people disabled by HIV disease.

Works by Lee Lynch

Toothpick House
Old Dyke Tales
The Swashbuckler
Home In Your Hands
Dusty's Queen of Hearts Diner
The Amazon Trail
Sue Slate, Private Eye

Chapter 1

A huge shadow appears on the wall outside my window. I slip my catnip stash back under my chair. As slow as a fish truck on Good Friday, the shadow creeps along the peeling white paint. It looks like some mangy type with revenge on his mind is giving me about thirty seconds to get my life in order.

I check my gray stripe suit and vest. If I am about to bite the litter, I prefer to do it spiffy. My saddle shoes still show the lick and polish of the shoeshine girl outside the Greasy Bowl Diner where I lunch. I tilt my fedora over my left eye.

As for my office, the shadow can take it or bury it. For the rent I pay, I am lucky to get a shelf to sit on, and this first-class view of Peacock Alley through a permanently open window. Sure it is drafty, but if there were glass in it how would my clients get in? The overall office decor is Early Cobweb à la Jackson Polecat. For a ground floor in San Francisco, delicately scented with mildew, this joint is not half bad.

As the shadow comes closer, I notice it is more elegant than sinister. It moves along like my ship coming in and stops short of the window. I hear a rustling sound, a jangle like bracelets. Just over the window's edge I see the very tip of a curling feather. All of a sudden I know this is no ruffian. This feather belongs to only one woman. My heart starts beating like three families of kittens playing on a tin roof.

Indeed, in one swift pounce Tallulah Mimosa is balancing on my windowsill. The fluttering of pigeons sounds like angel wings.

"I'm looking for Sue Slate, Private Eye," she says, her voice like a juicy purr.

I am meanwhile dragging air through a throat that feels like I march the Sahara round trip at high noon. This judy steps out of a dream I never even know I am having.

"At your service," I reply with a suave tone I keep handy for just such emergencies. Bowing, I am meanwhile disengaging from my former pounce stance in as graceful a manner as I can muster. I gesture to a clear patch of shelving for her to sit on.

And sit she does, like this is what she came for. Like she is paid to do it for a living. Like this is the greatest performance of her lives. I am spellbound as she lowers herself with a slinky sinuous move she does not learn at any Catlick school. She smooths her multi-colored jumpsuit — black, gold, cream — with a manicured paw. The left side of her face is solid black, a half-mask which dips down her nose like a roller coaster giving a thrill. It splashes across her delicate upper lip, her right cheek, and ends somewhere under the jumpsuit. Right at her neck, like an oversized piece of fourteen carat ice, is a flash of blinding white fur. She wears Roemance, the ritzy scent sold exclusively at Cats Fifth Avenue.

"You ought to be in real life, powder puff," I say under my breath, "you're too good for pictures."

She crosses her legs and lets the black one dangle. I thing she is putting the chill on me until I see that she is wringing those pretty paws. Still, there is something about a dame who wears mauve claw-polish that steams up my marbles. It takes me a while to catch on that the Camille act she is pulling is legit.

After this first detection of the day I am off and running like a nag carrying a betting jockey.

"How can I help you, sister?" I ask, hoping there is a nickel or two involved in rescuing this damsel in distress. I have about half that in my pocket and no prospects for more.

"Please," she says in the husky whisper that is so famous. "Can you help me?"

Most gumshoes would stand on their heads to help Tallulah Mimosa. I have a rep to maintain. I re-cock my hat and make like I am not holding onto my shelf.

You see, the lady is a torch singer. She performs right here at the Peacock Olley Cafe. To see her, the

3

cats crowd the back stairs and landings, the fire escapes and fence tops, the window sills and decks and roofs, like this is Madison Square Garden in Rocky Doublepaw's heyday. Last winter a very well-regarded producer graces the Alley with his presence and makes Ms. Mimosa the big offer. Six months later "Birdie Boogie" still tops the charts. I do not break down yet to see her act as my business ties me up at night, so to speak, but I often hear her from a distance when I work. I congratulate myself that the mountain finds her way to Mohammed.

"I am very glad to help you out, Ms. Mimosa," I say when I can trust my voice to sound professional.

Daintily, she licks a paw and uses it to wipe a tear from the tawny side of her face. I decide it is tacky to offer to help with this procedure also.

"It —" she starts, her voice breaking. "It's about —" She pauses again, dabs a hanky at her half-black nose. "About my kittens."

"Your kittens?" I ask with no little shock. I am of the impression that this pretty plays in my ball park from the word go and has no truck with breeder toms.

"Oh! You're taking me all wrong!" she says. I refrain from mentioning that I am not fussy how I take her. "I'm assuming too much. You don't know what happens. Please follow me, if you will."

I get up like a torched cannonball.

"But first," she says, laying a light paw on mine. This is the gentlest touch I ever experience. "I must tell you that I can't pay much for you to solve this crime."

I sit down. A woman's got to eat and this song and dance is as old as Raymond Chandler. I am what

4

you call a member of the fuppy — feline urban professionals — generation. I prefer the higher-priced spreads, rare cheeses, salmon out of season.

Tallulah Mimosa looks at me from her sweet almond eyes. "Everyone thinks the famous Tallulah Mimosa is rolling in the green these days, I know. But it's not like this. I sign on with the producer at a low rate of pay not daring to hope for more than his promises of fame and fortune. Olley pays me ten percent of the Cafe's take, but half the audience brings its own nip — and then Mom and Dad need help back in the vineyard." She fumbles in her purse. "Is this enough to start?"

I look down at the smacker, up at her. She bats those green worlds under her lashes. I shove the smacker back at her and jump to the sill. Some days I am just all heart.

"Let us take a gander," I say, and show her through the window.

Chapter 2

I follow Tallulah Mimosa down Peacock Alley.

Our resident mockingbird, Morty, flings her songs to the sky like an overwrought nickelodeon. All of a sudden she stops this serenade due to the loud pop of a firecracker nearby. Tallulah looks like she jumps half out of her jumpsuit. Fourth of July approaches like another shadow on my wall. Bangs and sizzles are quite popular, so to speak, with the local People. It is said that the only breed haughtier than the Siamese is People. They do not care about our

6

sensitive ears. Nor do they share our fastidious habits; their garbage chokes the Alley. I am no little embarrassed to walk here with Tallulah Mimosa. Yet over the smells of trash and fizgig powder, there is the faint spicy odor of sweet bay laurels which line the other side of the fence. The Coddess sets these bushes, and the red bottle brush flowers, and the bright lemon trees, along these alleyways to gild feline environs.

Tallulah Mimosa walks ahead. Her rump sashays one way, her long tail flicks the other and her back muscles ripple right down through her tail. I force my eyes to the ground.

She zips under a chain link fence and over a wooden one, tiptoes along a ledge and wiggles to a screen door right on the sidewalk. This lands us at a ground-floor pad. Indeed she is not in good circumstances. I am under the impression dames like her all rent penthouses complete with Abyssinian houseboys.

She inserts a delicate paw between the frame and the doorjamb and pulls then thrusts her haunch at the door to keep it open. I follow.

"Is that you, Patches?" calls a People with a voice which sounds not unlike a soft hand rubbing under my chin.

"Come on into my parlor, Big Girl," Tallulah tells me.

There is a shuffling. "Ah! You've brought home a friend! A little tom?" she asks in her loud voice. Then she gets closer to me. "No! It's Madonna, from across the alley."

I do not look in my dreamboat's eyes, preferring

7

to give up one of my lives before I let Tallulah Mimosa hear the name my People gives me. Madonna indeed.

"Any sign of the kittens?" asks Big Momma. A thousand wrinkles per square inch appear around the smile on her face.

Ms. Mimosa brushes against Big Momma, the salvation of many a feline destiny on Peacock Alley. Though previously once a racehorse trainer, she now has the weighty duty of managing two domiciles which flank the Alley. This she does in great earnestness, accepting no back talk from People regarding possessions, garbage or treatment of the furrier species.

Tallulah Mimosa bats her lashes at me. We leave Big Momma loudly discussing the events of the world with herself as she tends to a beefy pot on the stove.

"My little nook," says Ms. Mimosa, wrapping her tail around that lovely posterior as she settles on a pink satin pillow. I look twice at this object as it does not square with the lady's assessment of her lifestyle.

She gives it a lick. "This is presented to me by an admirer, much against my will. I place it on the trash heap several times, but poor Big Mom always gives it back. She is so confused to find it in the garbage that I finally give in to please her. Not that I don't enjoy it, Sue Slate. I just don't like to think about *him*."

She falls silent.

I decide that a show of my businesslike manners is appropriate now. "If it should be to your convenience, Ms. Mimosa, I should be pleased to hear about the kittens."

8

Her whiskers point downward, but then a twinkle comes into her masked eye. "First tell me, Sue Slate. Are you *always* such a mix of stiff formality and street butch?"

A series of convoluted replies take shape in my mind, but I am too acutely embarrassed to let them into the light of day.

"I don't ask this to upset you," she explains. "I find you charming right down to your bow-legged walk."

I try to examine my legs, but they are, as per usual, out of sight beneath me. Bow-legged?

She gives with a gentle laugh, then leans forward and places her little paw like a puff of fog on my arm. "May I call you Sue?"

"Yes, ma'am," I answer. I feel like a toasted mousemallow about to burst into glorious sugary flames.

"Tell me," she goes on, "how an educated woman like yourself gets into this private eye business?"

I am still puzzled by her choice of my attributes to admire, but I manage an explanation. "My People is a compulsive mystery reader," I explain. "Levis is even known to forget to feed us on the dots of eight A.M. and five P.M. due to this obsession. As a consequence, and especially near those hours, I learn the art of detection over Levis's shoulders. I am conversant with the methods of Georges Simenon and Raymond Chandler. When it is time to begin to earn my living it is only natural that I hang up a detective shingle."

"And wait for customers?"

"Indeed not. I serve my apprenticeship with the best lawcat in the West: Omar Sheriff of Texas. Some

9

time back she runs down a varmint to these parts and I volunteer as a deputy. Officer Sheriff recognizes my abilities immediately and sends me all her local referrals."

Ms. Mimosa has a way of looking fascinated, as if I am some such famed orator as Daniel Pawster, but it occurs to me that I am in the presence of a most desirable female lesbicat who appears to be deflecting me from my purpose. Can Tallulah Mimosa have something to hide?

"To return to the matter at paw, Ms. Mimosa," I intrude, composing myself, "do you have any indication of fowl play having to do with the aforementioned kittens?"

"It's a long story, Sue Slate, and as you perhaps can guess, I find it hard to bring myself to discuss it. Please bear with me." In a voice husky with unshed tears she adds, "You are most patient."

I have the distinct impression that patience is a virtue Ms. Mimosa appreciates at other times too.

She covers her eyes with her slender forearm. "It is too too horrible to think about!" She lowers her paw and breathes a ragged breath. "The poor kittens! You see, they're fathered by none other than the man who gives me this satin pillow. I never wish to consort with him, I tell him I am fey, yet he doesn't listen and presses his attentions on me. He tells me tales of woe. He is the adult kitten of a catniholic. He lives an abused childhood which leaves him scarred. Further rejection is unbearable to him. I take pity and allow him to visit me." She takes another labored breath. "Then he attempts to take advantage of me! Big Momma rescues me in the nip of time!"

I am forced to admit that at this point the furnace of my heart is fueled as much by this lady's suffering in the matter as by the tragic circumstance that brings us together.

She is reduced to a hoarse whisper. "One rainy night after work my accompanist is unable to escort me home. As I approach my door I hear pitiful mewlings. On my doorstep what do I find but three ragged, wet and dirty bundles of fur. They are in a shoebox whose cover isn't hard to lift and they greet me like I'm the legendary Wonderkitty riding to their rescue. Without further ado I bring them inside where, for two weeks, they fatten and thrive and drive Big Mom to distraction with their curtain-climbing antics."

After a pause wherein I chivalrously rid us of a pesty gnat, she goes on. "As each day goes by it becomes more and more obvious, Sue Slate, that these aren't just any kittens left on Big Mom's doorstep. All three are marked not unlike me, but with wavy fur. One has huge copper-colored butterfly wings across his back, another has four dark brown dress socks the shade of my tights, and the third wears a copper-colored beret. Big Mom looks at me inquisitively once or twice, but she knows I am never, thank goodness, pregnant. The copper coloring, and the wavy fur is the same as that cad, that cur, that horrid creature Big Mom so recently drives from our home —"

"Oh, no," I say, recognizing from the copper coloring our local Catanova. "Rex Boudoir!"

"None other!"

"And now?"

"They're gone! Our charges are kitnapped!"

Chapter 3

The lady succumbs to the boo hoos. I wish to aid and comfort her, but recognize that I am as smitten as a fly under a swatter, and not therefore to be trusted.

When the waterworks end I hide the tremor of my paws and return to my client. Sometimes it is very tough indeed to be a hard-boiled detective.

"How do you happen to discover this despicable situation?" I ask.

Does a desperate panic cross her features? Her hat

shades the side of her face that is not masked, like a veiled lady. In my business, silence implies guilt.

"They're taken some time in the night, Sue Slate."

"Surely you hear sounds, commotions?"

She casts her green orbs to the floor. "I'm sorry, but I'm fatigued last evening. My work takes a great deal out of me."

"Big Mom? She hears nothing?"

"She assumes it is only the kittens playing and falls back to sleep dreaming of elderly, well-behaved cats."

I promote a tour of the kittens' basket, food bowls and other places where a clue might linger, but the tracks are cold. Nothing is out of place and there is no sign of struggle.

"Ah-ha," I say. Is the perpetrator known to the kittens?

"I must take my departure now, Ms. Mimosa, to have a look-see outside."

She asks, "May I come with you?"

I take another goggle at this firm-footed pretty and pick up on the toughness that gets her where she is today. I determine that she is capable of looking after herselves.

Outside, young People yell, buses slide on overhead lines, trolleys roll on tracks, and the city is lousy with rubber wheels rubbing up and down the hills.

We climb wood stairs and porches, descend down the fire escapes, fight through brooms and flower pots and picnic coolers. We check out every doorway and windowsill with no clue as to the whereabouts of said kittens. At my window I see my People, Levis,

14

preening. I know his name is Levis because he always wears a tag to this effect on the back of his jeans. He is gray-haired with a shaggy moustache and talks as fast as a hummingbird bats her wings. In order to earn catfood he teaches something called chem mystery.

Through the bedroom window I espy Darlin', Levis's long time squeeze. He is a small, soft-voiced People, with skin not quite as black as Hot Paw's tux. He does not wear a name tag, but Levis always calls him Darlin'. Once he is mater dee at a fancy cook shack, but he has something akin to the Feline Leukemia Virus which rips through Peacock Alley now and then, felling many of our dear ones.

When Darlin' spots us in the window he gives a weak high five. I know he is not in on this kitnapping business as I spend last night with him until Levis gets home. He is lonely and sick and needs a pal. But there is no way I am owning to Tallulah that I play nursey-nursey. If this kind of poop hits the streets my image is ruined.

My investigatory route leads me past some places of no interest and then to the Computer Moll's pad. The Moll has mega-short black hair which exposes an earring collection that jingles and shines so much she is like a walking mobile. Her bird Dolly Parrot is a loud nasty type who lives in a floor-to-ceiling palace. When the Moll's girlfriend runs off with another woman, the Moll adopts a computer named Alice. The word is that she is either throwing herself into work with Alice, or can be heard sobbing through the night as a result of broken-heart-i-tis. However, despite repeated assiduous attempts, no one ever deciphers exactly what work it is that the Moll does.

15

Her pad is always locked too tight to investigate, with chains and bolts and padlocks, like she is suspicious someone cares to harm Alice or her grody old bird. As a matter of record, if ever there is a window open the line of felines with birdycide on their minds in all likelihood would extend across 14th Street.

"Ah-ha!" I say to Ms. Mimosa. "The kitchen window is unlocked!"

Tallulah looks like the kitnapper is about to jump out at us. "Does that mean something?" she asks.

"In this business, Sweet Lips, something can mean nothing, but nothing always means something."

The judy twitches her tawny tail. "You're too cute for words, Sue Slate, Private Eye."

Cute? Private eyes are *not* cute. Can this Tallulah Mimosa mock *me*, Sue Slate? Does she seek to distract me from my duties? Or, perhaps she sincerely thinks I am devastating.

I tilt my fedora and climb. Tallulah Mimosa is about to learn what happens when Sue Slate points her tail. At the top of the stairs, a hungry sun laps fog from the bowl of the city.

As far as I can see, white buildings overlap white buildings. Seagulls mew like kittens. Smells of flowers and fruiting trees fill the tiny gardens. My heart softens toward Ms. Mimosa. With her beside me I feel like I can fly, like she may burst into song, like heaven is just down the hall.

We jump as several firepoppers explode in the street. Pigeons lift from every rooftop like girls in a fun house. Then I notice a strange scent that is nothing like orange blossoms.

"Wait here."

Tallulah blinks her velvety lashes. "I want to come with you, Sue."

This dame sticks to me like a burr in summer. I ponder why a success story like Ms. Birdie Boogie Herself pays a private eye to keep her company. I call into the apartment whence the stench emits. When no answer is forthcoming, I enter.

Big Ole lives here. He is a gargantuan nurse, round as Santy Cat, and has a ring of yellow hair around his bald pate. Also, he is known for his laughing eyes, in which I do not recently see any laughter. He is always good for a pawout, and I am of the opinion that he can harm no living thing.

The place gets even whiffier. It is a wreck. His mattress is flipped off the bed, his dresser drawers are emptied, his uniforms are tossed. This is quite unusual as Big Ole is reputed to be the neatest People in San Francisco. Even his porch is empty of junk.

I feel Ms. Mimosa's hip brush mine. Her eyes are quite large with fright.

Side by side we creep toward the bathroom.

"Leapin' lesbicats!" cries Ms. Mimosa.

I put my tail around her. Big Ole is laid out flat on the floor, parallel to the bathtub, face flat down in blood, like he falls forward and breaks his nose. His hands are to his sides. I sniff the back of his head: something hits him there, hard. He is not breathing. In his fall he knocks a bottle of perfume to the floor. This is the odor which alerts me to the evildoing.

"Perfume?" I query.

"What's wrong? Is he drunk?" asked Ms. Mimosa.

"I never see him in a state of inebriation in my life."

"Perhaps he slips getting out of the tub?"

"Where is the water? Why is he wearing all his clothes?"

"He passes out from hunger."

"A People that size? In addition, his breakfast dishes are empty on the kitchen table."

"Then you think —"

"Big Ole is dead."

"Oh, no!"

"And it is no accident. One does not hit the back of one's head while falling flat on one's face — unless someone else does the hitting."

"Maybe he is frolicking with a friend and gets pushed by mistake."

"A friend would call in the sirens."

"Then what —"

"With all due respect, Ms. Mimosa, I am *processing*." She looks at me with awe-filled eyes and falls silent. This is definitely my kind of woman.

"Another thing that bothers me," I tell her after a while. "Big Ole is once gay. He is a major camp artist in those days. Then he is born again and out go the dresses. Why does he have perfume in his bathroom now?"

"Perhaps it's a man's cologne like 'English Feather.' "

I kick the bottle over. " 'Obsession.' Is it possible that he douses himself with 'Obsession' pursuant to returning to the gay life, a fallen born-again — and that his Cod strikes him dead?"

"I don't know about that, Sue —"

"You are right, Ms. Mimosa. I am afraid we must face the fact that he is —"

"Murdered!" she sobs.

I am ready to soothe her, but I see that her emotion is not fear, it is anger.

"What an odious criminal!" she exclaims. "The kittens stolen from the only home they ever knew and now this! Killing a People who's as gentle as a kitten. Who could want to do this?"

We turn to face the apartment.

"The place is ransacked," I answer. "But not by some two-bit goniff with a habit to support. This is a search."

Big Ole is still warm. I sniff around, trying to detect something besides his "Obsession." His magazines are rifled, videos unreeled, cushions slashed, curtain hems ripped open, mirrors pulled off walls, food dumped from canisters and boxes. The only thing left undisturbed is the back hall wherein laundry paraphernalia sits beside a water heater. The heater looks like a bag lady wrapped in tattered insulation.

Ms. Mimosa no longer keeps it together. She makes like a palm tree in a hurricane. Her teeth chatter so loud I hear them across the room. I nobly nudge her to the back hall. Once more, the slack wrapping on the water heater draws my eyes. Something obtrudes below its edge.

Just at that moment Tallulah Mimosa jumps as if the mouse revolution begins. Her quaking paw points to the front door. Then I hear it: a great thundering

19

of footsteps. A pounding begins. I grab for the hanging object and at the same time propel the judy outside.

"Open up! Po-lice!" screams a ferocious People. Then the door bursts in.

Chapter 4

By the time the enormous Alice Blue Gown thrusts his head onto Big Ole's porch, Tallulah Mimosa and I sun ourselves like innocent babes.

"Nothing but some old tomcats," he shouts back inside.

With one eye I see my lady friend's back fur rise at this comment. With the other I am examining the cardboard, plastic and film object I hide by flinging myself onto it. What is this gizmo I pull from the insulation? Can it be what the intruders seek?

We make our way down the steps. At the bottom

Ms. Mimosa turns toward me. I note that seductive look in her eye, the batting eyelashes, the strange tense kink in her tail. She is asking to be kissed. I move toward her, she sways toward me. My breath gets stuck around my third rib. Can she hear my heart throb? I lean to kiss her.

Then I see them, in the crack of the sidewalk at Ms. Mimosa's feet: two sparkling rhinestones exactly at the bottom of Big Ole's steps.

"Sue?" Tallulah whispers expectantly. Her eyes are still closed, her nose twitching in anticipation of the kiss.

"Whoops," I say to myself, for this is a lovely sight indeed. However, work before pleasure. I scoop up the rhinestones and pocket them. Tallulah appears to sigh. Alas, the moment is lost. I escort my leading lady home.

"Can I expect a report on your progress?" she asks. This is not the poised pretty I first set eyes on this A.M.

"You can bet your sexy whiskers," I promise and set off to smoke out my brother.

As per the usual I locate him shooting a dice game called Rats and Mice in the back of Peacock Olley Cafe. He is looking about as spiffy as a moldy statue in his snap-brim cap with a bird stain smack in its center. Since our last meeting he adds a new broken whisker to his collection and sports an ear at half-mast. This reminds me to say my prayer of gratitude that I am born first.

I arrive in this world one minute prior to him. Mom, bless her padded soles, gloms a kid's broken blackboard at this moment and I get the moniker Slate. When she opens her orbs after my brother's

22

entrance she sees a dumpster. As soon as he is old enough to choose a first name he attempts to dignify his misfortune: Demetrius Dumpster Esquire.

He is also born with a stomach for a brain and at the moment indulges his two greatest passions: gambling for mousesteaks.

"Hey, Dumpster," I say.

"It's your sister, Demetrius dear," whispers Turtle Dove.

Turtle Dove is Dumpster's old lady, a drag queen who dresses out of the best trash cans, but always ends up with the dregs which at one time adorn the backs of ladies who decorate their walls with black velvet portraits of Bambi. Thus her normal attire consists of a gold lamé jumpsuit.

However, as Turtle Dove lives in awe of me for rescuing her from Bad Tuna Gat's gang, I live and let live.

Dumpster growls at her. "I know my own damn sister."

"But, dear —" Turtle Dove says. She fusses with her pink patent-leather collar.

"Can't you see I'm busy? Or are you feeding *yourself* tonight, you dewinged fairy!"

"I am only trying to remind you, Demetrius, that you already win four mouse steaks and are supposed to be watching your waistline. Think of all that cholesterol."

"So I'm hungry. So arrest me."

Turtle Dove lets out an unearthly yowl, as per usual, when I charge and land on Dumpster's back.

Dumpster rises like a bucking horse and carries on in quite an undignified manner. He is three-legged and lists even more than usual when I ride him. He swats at me with his terminally scuffed white bucks. When I let him go he charges. I hold him at leg's length, one filthy paw flailing at me like a windmill in a storm. In the meanwhile I fill him in on the details of the crimes we must solve.

"We?" he shouts. "You mean while I do all the dirty work and you get all the glory?" My brother's disposition is not of the highest order. He is like this ever since losing his back leg in the wars, an event about which he will not let the dog out of the bag.

"How you paying, Sis? You taking us to Liverland for baskets of McGizzards?"

"Pay he wants? Pay when three little kittens are lost in the world without a soul to care about them? Can you not contemplate anything but next Tuesday's breakfast?"

"Next Tuesday?" he says, his eyes lustering up like a catnip tree on Solstice Eve.

Before I can bean the boy, Turtle Dove intervenes. "I have a new one for you, Sue! Listen! How does a witch spell mousetrap?"

Turtle Dove's passion is for riddles.

"Give up? C-A-T!"

I groan and issue instructions to Dumpster to dig up whatever he can find on the crimes.

All this gustatory discussion reminds me that I am famished. I wend my way home where I discover that Dumpster already hits the bowls with his thirty strawpower tongue. However, Levis forgets to put away the breakfast butter. I glance in the bedroom to ascertain that Darlin' is sleeping, then dig my cache of anchovy sauce out from behind the electric heater. Poured over butter it makes a scrumptious meal.

Sucking little anchovy bones from between my

teeth, I retire to my library. I am halfway through an Agatha Kitty, but it is not as lively as I like them. I hug my teddy dog to me, and join Darlin' in nod-out land.

It is late afternoon when I awaken to the sounds of Fred and Ginger Backstair, the tapdancing cats, in full rehearsal on the floor above me. After counting 73,012 taps I haul myself out of bed. Duty calls. Life is unfair; it is my business to try and even the score. A hard and cold business, but I can take it.

Just then Levis arrives home. Dumpster pushes past him through the door, yowling.

"Is little Sting a hungry kitty?" Levis asks. "and how about Madonna?"

I take one look at the lizard goulash he dumps out of a can and turn tail, leaving Dumpster, who has no shame, to siphon it up.

Before venturing into the Alley, I determine to study my find from the water heater once more. I pull it out from its hiding place under the rug.

Levis comes out of the kitchen.

"Madonna! Where did you get that?"

He advances on me. His behavior tells me that I am not supposed to be in possession of this trophy. Levis bends to confiscate it. I roll on my back and fling it away from him.

"That's not a toy, kitty," says Levis, his words running together in his usual haste. "It could represent years of someone's work."

Oh yeah? Then why is it stuffed up a water heater?

"What's going on?" calls Darlin' softly.

"Did you see what these cats are playing with, darlin'?"

25

"No, what?"

Levis makes a surprise grab for it, but I snag it toot sweet. I make a combination of cute moves and that darned cat plaything just happens to slide right under the purple couch.

"You infuriating little tiger!" says Levis.

"Where in the world did she get a computer disk?" Darlin' asks. Levis goes to hug him.

Ah-ha! I make like I am bird-dogging the thing until I get it stashed back under the rug. So it is a computer disk. Can it belong to the Computer Moll? Does this connect her with Big Ole?

Chapter 5

The population which twilight lures from Peacock Alley is quite something else. I take my evening stroll at this time in order to keep up with neighborhood events.

Three Elder cats, slow and balding, stroll in front of me. They brag regarding their actions in the great gang wars between the Razzmatazz Katz from Dolores Street and the Lowlifes from Guererra.

Several moms chew the rag in a doorway while they watch their fuzzy kittens climb all over each other. I check the kittens out: no copper-colored butterfly wings, no brown dress socks, no copper-colored berets.

Under a fire escape a shaggy-furred adolescent type hawks pamphlets from the Feline Potential Movement.

Members of The Scavengers, a gang that follows garbage trucks, sell junk from their last haul. One of this lot looks like he contemplates a negative comment upon my androgynous appearance, but I freeze him nearly dead with my paralyzer grin.

I climb the rusty fire escape. The last light catches on the fog banks and rolls inland. Eucalyptus trees rattle their shiny leaves like streetwalkers shaking their stuff. I think of the kittens and wonder if they live to enjoy all this. However, I cannot afford to go soft on them. I have work to do.

At Big Ole's pad I squeeze in through the hole behind the water heater. The gendarmes leave every other entry sealed like death can be quarantined. I sniff out the whole joint at my leisure, but the big police feet jumble all the scents and I soon throw in the towel. Outside again I see this is not my night, to say the least.

Who should be leaning against the railing, chomping on some dog's half-chewed rawhide stogie, but my dearest sibling Dumpster. Turtle Dove's fur is spiked up punk style. She nibbles at the claws on her hind feet.

"You two are a sight for sore eyes."

"Who you calling an eyesore?" Dumpster asks.

"Oh, Demetrius, give your sister a chance," says Turtle Dove.

Dumpster inspects his slimy stogie. "I hear you scout me out again." He squints at me over it. "So,

Sis? Parley voo." This is a phrase he picks up from Justine, a poodle neighbor.

I traditionally signal my desire to discuss important matters with him by placing a stogie under his cushion at Levis's pad. This I do after my nap today.

"I must effect an entry to the Computer Moll's lodging," I inform them.

He looks at the sky. "Are you kidding? That place is done up tighter than a carrier on the way to the vet's. Besides, it's about time for my twilight snack." He sighs. "I love food. You want to know why? I am never hungry after I eat."

"This is the kitten caper, bro'. Your pot-belly-thon can wait."

"You sure the Moll ain't at home?"

"No. I am trying to get caught, toadbrain. I need you to keep the fool parrot distracted in order that she does not alert the whole Alley to my investigation. And I happen to know a window is mysteriously left open these days."

Turtle Dove files her claws on the iron railing.

"And no rough stuff, buckarubies. Just distract her."

"I can take care of the bird," says Turtle Dove.

"This is what I am afraid of," I say, looking at her claws.

"Oh, Blanche," chides Turtle Dove. "I don't do S&M. Dolly Parrot simply adores my riddles! I can distract her, no panting. How's this for starters —"

I attempt to fling myself down the stairs, but she is right after me.

"A hunky tom says to his lady —" She begins to giggle. "Says to her — and listen, her whiskers are

29

all up in rollers, the kittens are screaming for their chow, they're having a fight because the tom blows his week's pay on a game of Old Spayed —" Turtle Dove begins to lose it here. Tears roll down her muttonchops. "He says to her, *You musta been a horse in your last life, 'cause you're sure a nag now!*"

I give her my paralyzer grin, but she is laughing too hard to notice. We are outside the Computer Moll's. "What do you say, Dump, I know the bird is a feather-brain, but I don't see her going for the jokester. Do you think you can pull off this number?"

"Rain de toot," he says and limps off toward the Computer Moll's.

Immediately thereafter I learn that this Dolly Parrot is indeed of the same bird-brained mentality as Turtle Dove. She shrieks with laughter at the Dove's riddles while I venture inside.

There are family photographs everywhere, which I find strange as I never see any of these people in the vicinity, nor does the Computer Moll seem to leave the premises long enough to go visiting. It is a large Chinese family, living, I deduce from the backgrounds, here in San Francisco. The Moll looks to be the eldest daughter. What happens to estrange her from them? Is this another reason she cries and locks herself up from the world? Such isolation can turn her bitter and hateful as I know from certain cat acquaintances.

Before effecting entry, I recover the disk I had previously stashed under a flower pot. Not familiar with this type widget, I am long since decided to treat it with respect. Now I wield it as I advance on Alice the Computer with much stealth.

"Ah-hem," I say. "Good day, Ms. Alice. Allow me

to introduce myself. I am the, uh, the rodent exterminator, hired by the Computer Moll in order to rid your domicile of pests."

Alice does not answer.

I jump to her chair and meet my first obstacle. The chair lurches and spins. I am deposited under the desk. This annoys me no end. I pick myself and my disk up and, with an intimidating growl, charge the desk.

Alice just sits there.

I approach cautiously and give her a sniff. She does not appear to be bothered by this intimacy. I hear Turtle Dove outside ratting through her riddle repertoire. I take a deep breath in order to calm myself and nudge Alice with my nose.

Nothing.

I rub against her, slap my tail on her, caterwaul at her. This thingamajigit is getting my goat. I leap onto her keys. But these do not make marks like the keys on Levi's typewriter. Do they signal the cavalry or some such?

I do a little dance across the keys. Q U E E R K I T T Y, I tap out. Then, ! @ # $ % ^ & * ( ) _ + = ~ ' \ | ; : " ' ? / . , [ ] { } ! That ought to tell her.

Someone coughs. I nearly jump out of my saddle shoes, but it is only a People next door. Then I spot the plastic box. I nudge the top open. Ah-ha! It is filled with disks just like the one I carry. Now we get somewhere.

HIV Kansas City reads the first. The second reads *HIV Tucson*. The third, *HIV Paris*. I check mine. It is blank. What can these initials mean? And the cities? This is a puzzle indeed.

31

I hop off the desk and investigate the Computer Moll's apartment. Aside from the fact that it looks like a family album, there are only the usual gay lib posters, pictures of girl People in bed with girl People, paintings of enormous bright birds — and an earring collection that takes over the bedroom. I peruse the books: *Pharmacology, Using MS-DOS, Understanding Chemistry, Beginning French, Experimental Medicine.*

Meanwhile Dolly begins to recite a blood-curdling rhyme for the benefit of Turtle Dove.

Fee, fi, foe, fat,
I smell the blood of a Kitty-Cat!
Be he plump
Or be he lean
Offa him will I dene!

I fear that this is all too tlrue as I toss aside my fedora and check my Mickey Mouse watch. The Computer Moll is not due home for hours and I have much work to do.

"Hey, Dolly! I got another one! Hot off the press! What animal drives a car? No. No! *No!* You'd never guess! A *road hog!* Get it?"

I move while the bird caws at its loudest. On a shelf beyond the desk lies a pile of papers. Each sheet is covered with formulas, which fact I know as a result of living with Levis. His chem mystery books are filled with formulas.

Then I find the letter.

Dear Jeff, it says. *We received your compilation of the experiments from London and Vienna. It's brilliant work and gives our little cadre of gay researchers*

32

great hope. We have duplicated the experiment and confirm that it works. Now to go on to the next step. I understand that Paris thinks we are close to the human experimentation stage. Have you consulted with the attorneys yet about how we can go about this outside the regular channels without getting sent to prison if something goes wrong? It would be a shame to lose all we've gained on this horrid disease and have to rely on the governments to come up with a cure. Will write again when we have more progress to report. In Gayspirit, Rog.

Well, I think. Well. What is this grand scheme upon which I stumble? What cure do they seek? Is it to Darlin's illness?

I am hot to trot. Is there more information? I feel a tingle at the base of my tail which announces I am on the right track.

On the next shelf are more papers. I leap to them, but the second that I land I know this is one wrong move. The paper slides under my paw. My paws slide back as I lean forward. I grab for an anchor, but my claws find nothing to hold. I am not much surprised, then, to find myself wishing for wings as I fly toward the floor, sheets of paper floating around me like giant snowflakes. The landing is soft, but the paper storm goes on and on. Turtle Dove's riddle ends and then there is silence except for paper sliding down, down, down, and my hopes for a clean getaway sink with them.

I am prudently extricating myself from this avalanche when I hear a buzz not unlike that of a kamakitty pilot coming in for a landing. On my head.

With a screech of her voice brakes, Dolly Parrot, whose cage door is always left ajar, lunges, but this is the moment I fling myself from the wreckage. She banks and comes at me again, flapping those wings like she remembers how to fly. In the moment before her descent I think, this is no parrot, this is a blitz bird. Then she is upon me, pecking at my coconut with a beak kept sharp for just such an eventuality.

I regret my fedora's placement across the room. I long to disengage my paws from protecting my head so that I can tear the stuffing out of Dolly. I yearn for my brother to avenge me. Mostly, though, I wish I am elsewhere.

Then I hear a sound never before welcome in all my years.

"Hey, Doll! Here's the best one saved for last! Watch out it doesn't knock you over! Listen! What does a drag kitty use to snare a rabbit dinner?"

"Caa-aw?" croaks Dolly, still clinging to me, but taking a peck break.

"Give up, you guano-head? A hare-net!" And Turtle Dove pounces on the bird, brandishing a hairnet, getting her claws and beak entangled in it just long enough for us to flee.

"Thanks, Dove," I say on the windowsill as I slip the disk back under my hatband.

"Rain de toot," answers Dumpster.

My head hurts too excessively for me to give him the evil eye.

"Caaaaaa-aaaaaaw!" It is indeed a battle cry from inside. I know we are goners if our getaway is not more swift than an Olympian puma's. Dolly's scream echoes through the Alley. We dive off the windowsill as she comes in for another landing.

Chapter 6

Dumpster, Turtle Dove and yours truly land under the furry cloak of darkness to streak down the fire escape. In the Alley we mingle with the crowd. Ferny linden trees screen us from the upstairs view and give the strip a jungly air. From down here, Doll sounds like a street vendor hawking the feathers that rain from her window.

I stop at a cart and buy a shot of milky. My paws shake. Calmer, I look around. The Alley is thick with the excitement of those who worship Tallulah Mimosa of which there are plenty. Everything smells like damp trash and sweet vegetation. Up the street goes a motorcycle like a flotilla of motorboats.

"Humph," I hear as I pass the last window of the Cafe. "Humph."

"What is the poop, Humphrey?" I jump up beside this portly blue-eyed Elder in his spotless white suit. His tail goes like a drumstick to the sound of the warm-up combo just getting into gear onstage.

"Humph," he says.

I reach into my vest pocket and slip him a fin.

"Humph," he says in satisfaction. "Notice anything out on the street?"

A seasoned bookie who teaches his art at the Catlick School, this Elder knows everything and everyone. One after another, customers drift over, and Humphrey takes odds on how many songs Tallulah Mimosa sings tonight.

"Nix, Humphrey. Something I ought to know?"

"The God Is Not Dead is hopping."

"On a Saturday night?"

He gives me an inscrutable look. The God Is Not Dead is the religious institution across the street, a straight-laced cinderblock affair squashed between gussied-up Victorians. It flaunts a neon cross that reads *God Is Not Dead*.

"Some characters over there in suits and ties, fork out hogwash about Sodom and Gomorrah where I understand a good time is had by all except some sore sports who are unlikely to enjoy themselves anywhere."

Like a flock of gabbling stiff-necked geese looking for a warm holyland, the congregation frequents our street only on Sundays. They descend from the burbs to which they long ago flee from faggots and dykes and queers and Mexicans and Asians and blacks and punks and every other group that is not just like them. They act like the newcomers to the neighborhood infest the homes they once occupy.

"Sourpeople," hisses Humphrey. "I hope they don't disrupt the festivities this evening as I am carrying a lot of bets on a long show. Humph."

Indeed, as I watch, the Alley becomes even more full. Cats who don their best furs for the occasion crowd onto steps and windowsills and fencetops. I wave some cash at Olley, owner of Peacock Olley Cafe, and she grins under her thatch of yellow and brown striped hair. She slides a glass of cold nip ale down the length of the bar. I tip my topper to Humphrey with thanks and leave him. His observation requires rumination on my part. At last sight *he* is ruminating on his fin.

The stage is a raised platform that juts out below the second story hallway window. I lean on a rail and watch the All-Edison Electric Orchestra, in tuxedos, swing into "Steppin' Out With My Baby." Fred and Ginger Backstair tap into view. The applause gets rowdy. The drummer, a tiny, black-jerseyed, white-gloved baby butch named Hot Paws, works up a sweat behind them. At the piano Woogie, Tallulah Mimosa's accompanist, flails his hairy gray Persian arms. Spooky round eyes look out from his gray face like yellow suns. Woogie is in love with Ms. Mimosa and is broken-hearted that she is gay.

I contemplate the singer somewhere in the dark shadows readying herself with Roemance and a ruffled gown. The Backstair duo finishes to hoots and hollers. My tail tingles when the drummer starts her tattoo. Woogie sits with pads poised over his keys. A stagepaw throws a blue cloth over the floodlight that is aimed at the stage. A jungle mural painted long ago by hippie People is the backdrop. Bright fruits hang from tropical trees. Lynxes, ocelots, pumas and jaguars, our proud foremothers. There is no sound now but Hot Paw's soft drumming.

Then, slinking from a dark corner of the stage, Tallulah Mimosa appears in a long multi-colored gown. One white haunch peeks out from a slit in the darker colors.

A lime-green scarf the color of her eyes trails behind her as she struts across the stage, swinging those hips to Woogie's impassioned intro into "An Affair To Remember." This is her theme song. As I watch this queen of all cats, I know it is my song too. The audience lets out a yowl that brings People to their windows.

Tallulah Mimosa begins to sing and the crowd falls silent as little cat feet. I berate myself. How foolish I am in the past, lying in my lonely bed listening while the fruit flies soar overhead instead of this coddess. I am hypnotized all through the first number.

Then I recall the other reason I am here.

I scan the throng. Who witnesses the kitnapping? Who knows why Big Ole gets knocked off? Does any cat know why the disk is so important?

Against the bar slouches the elegant Rex Boudoir of whom Ms. Mimosa so recently tells a tale. He is long and lean and rakish. His close-cropped wavy fur gleams. Personally, I am of the opinion that he glosses it with halibut-liver oil. Its coppery color reminds me that at least two of the kitnap victims are his progeny. Rex's unclaimed kits are causing a population crisis of no small dimension for years. Most of the gang members have Boudoir blood in their veins.

This Catanova is irresistible to the ladies. He has only one fatal flaw: his collar. Mrs. Kling, his People, provides this. She is a large woman, a nurse, but so full of stuffing she struts around like royalty. She is scared spitless that riffraff cats can enter her abode so she installs a door for Rex which opens only by means of a magnet in his rhinestone-studded collar. This magnet has a habit of attracting to itself every bit of scrap metal in the Alley. Rex spends all of his hours out of bed kicking paper clips off his collar in order so as not to look like a junked satellite.

The dancing begins on any hunk of cement that is free. I see Turtle Dove yank Dumpster into a bunny hop. Down the Alley two lines do the Prowl.

I lay my glims on Leonora, in a silver and black stripe pant suit. She is president of the Feline Potential Movement. Always she is adopting cute, scruffy young things not long out of school. Yellow Ethel is her latest rescue. Before Ethel drops out of Catlick School she attends only when the truant officer catches up with her. When she is in school rumor has it that the kid peddles so much soaked nip Feline Herstory class looks like a kittigarten class at nap time.

Soaked nip, for the elucidation of the general public, is very extremely illegal. The process by which a mere herb attains to this stature is one in which a soaker submerges a quantity of catnip in a liquid, then dries it. Some like it soaked in milky which is said to produce quite a mellow high. Some like it soaked in People liquors, which more than once causes a level-eared kitizen to flip her lid. Some like it steeped in the same water as other weeds. However, when this process is overseen by profit-mad crooks, then anything goes. It is impossible to discern if a batch of nip can produce euphoria or a more lethal consequence. Yet in the crowded alleys, young cats play Russian Blue Roulette for the thrill of it.

Ms. Mimosa brings tears to every eye as she sings "Climb Every Curtain."

Almost every eye. Atop a trash can Bad Tuna Gat beats time with his club-like tail. He is barrel-chested and when upright, has a floor-duster stomach. Tufts of dirty white fur belch out of his gray ears. He is an educated cat who teaches kitty lit at one time. However, soon after the early demise of his mother, to whom he is inordinately attached, he becomes hooked on nip and begins to sell the stuff to support his habit, then turns to other crime to protect his deals until he is enmeshed in a web of crime from which he cannot cut loose.

At the moment Bad Tuna stares at Yellow Ethel. It is likely that she deals for him. First he hooks the young ones, then he turns them loose to sell. The thought of this fallen intellectual makes my skin crawl. As a matter of fact, I recall that the last time I am forced to breathe the same air as this miscreant, he is holed up on Big Ole's porch, in hiding among chicken bones, milky-scummed saucers, and a ratty blanket filthy with shed gray furs.

I approach him on his sordid perch, then leap beside him on the trash can lid.

He glowers. "This is private property, shemale."

"Ah-ha! So Bad Tuna is investing in condobiniums now."

"Don't pull your fancy talk on me. I know you're nothing but a perverted finger artist."

"I am not here to quibble over who is the pervert, you walking dust-ball. I want to know since when you move in on Big Ole and what you have to do with the murder."

He pulls a tuft of grass from between his toes. His voice is as nonchalant as a bluejay who knows the cat wears a bell. "Why, I move out last week, Sue Slate. I have nothing to do with this criminal act."

"And I am a blue-ribbon show cat."

This four-legged vulture turns mean again. "Listen here, lez, you have no right to shove your sticky nose in my affairs. Make tracks or you are dogfood."

"Your mom would be real proud of her sleazeball son, would she not?" He lunges as I nimbly jump to the asphalt. "You are up to your whiskers in this mess, Tuna, and I plan to find out how." With a hiss, he takes a vicious swipe at me, but I elude it.

It is time for Tallulah Mimosa's big production number. Hot Paws rumbles while Woogie comes in at the low end of the keys. The chorus birds, in sleek black caps and green and yellow feathered short-shorts, do a tippy-toed jog onto the stage. Tallulah Mimosa sings her Goldfish Record, "Birdie Boogie." Behind her, the crooning birds kick up their skinny little legs, wings outspread. The audience makes like V-Day is here again.

Shimmying and scatting and boogeying and moaning, Tallulah Mimosa sings like she can move the universe. Let there be no doubt that she does indeed move my universe. I flash back on my last love, little Trixie.

41

A good girl, my strawberry blonde, she is around just long enough for me to get used to her. Then one night I show up at her place a little worse for the wear after a thirty-six-hour stakeout and a run-in with a gang of flounderheads. Trixie is there for me. She pastes balm on my wounds, pours love on my frazzled soul.

I awake the next morning to find her gonzo. The note on her pillow reads, *My dearest Sue, I can never love another. I cannot bear to leave, but neither can I stand to keep putting you back together. I depart forever this tragic day, but I leave my heart behind.*

I open my eyes now. Tallulah Mimosa looks to sing a blues number directly to me. And she sings the blues like they are her best friend. Maybe, I surmise, maybe what this private eye needs, is not a homebody like little Trixie, but a working girl like myself. A woman with her own scars and a need to be free as a wildcat.

She towers over the birdy line as she dances with them, yet she is as light on her paws as they are on their spindly gams. Her green eyes blaze with passion from under her half-mask. Does she look the way of yours truly? Fireworks go off somewhere up toward the park. Additionally somewhere inside my head.

From the corner of my eye I catch a furtive movement on the steps across the yard. Just then Tallulah switches tempo and swings into a sultry rendition of "A Foggy Day In Peacock Alley." I forget everything but Tallulah Mimosa.

Chapter 7

If there is one thing I am expert at in this life, it is to sleep the sleep of the just. However, what with my aching bones after Dolly Parrot's assault, the bonfire Ms. Mimosa's songs touch off in my heart and the caterwauling she inspires down in the Alley, as well as the third degree I am giving myself about this case, I am doing the toss and turn all night between Levis and Darlin'.

Do not take it wrong that I sometimes spend my nights counting sheep with my People. For one thing, somekitty has to, Dumpster is not always willing to give up his nocturnal pleasures. For another, though I am no nursey-nursey, Darlin' has some nights I do not wish on a dog and Levis needs his sleep in order to go out and earn catfood the following day.

So this night I curl up against Darlin's head and pretend his hair is Tallulah Mimosa. He is restless, though, and every time he turns I wake with a memory of the furtive type whom I see skulking on the fire escape at the concert. Who could it be? Why do they spy on the cabaret? Or am I just getting carried away and seeing enemies in every corner?

When the sun creeps over the windowsill it is of a golden hue not unlike the gold in Ms. Mimosa's coat. I lie staring into it with longing while Darlin' struggles into the shower and through the ordeal of his innumerable medications, too proud to wake Levis for help. I make haste to exit before he uses the last of his energy to open a can of cat food.

On the fire escape I do my workout, stretching my muscles into the keen alertness necessary to my profession. I hone my claws to dangerous points. All around are light-colored buildings, glaring in the sun, and porches for miles filled with flower pots and blossoms of wondrous variety. Stairs, rails and clotheslines crisscross like giant spiderwebs. I take in a deep breath of air tangy with salty water. Morty Mockingbird greets the day with a medley. The sordid San Francisco night of lustful toms and murder might not exist. But Sue Slate, Private Eye, cannot ignore the fact that they do.

I stop by Tallulah Mimosa's to report in, but there is no sign of her even this early in the A.M. I find this strange as she is purported on the grapevine to be canned goods at the moment, that is, on the shelf.

Miss Kitty is my next stop. Even more of an elder than Humphrey, Miss Kitty roosts on her back porch where she surveys every angle of the Alley. It is generally useful to pump her and also she likes the company.

I am halfway up her steps when she calls out, "Yoo-hoo! Is that Sue Slate, the albacore of my eye? You get that handsome stripey body up here!"

So much for undercover work, I think, although I am invited under Miss Kitty's covers more than once.

Her freshly fluffed tail pats a space on the rag rug beside her. Makeup rings her eyes so heavily she looks not unlike a raccoon.

"Sit down, my dear, sit down," she says. "It's a Maine Coon's age since I last saw you. I suppose this is as usual a business visit? I can't offer you a sip of milky as Ethan is out partying again last night and *forgets* it. Men!"

I catch the way she bats her eyelashes and survey the remainder of her while she goes on about her People Ethan, a good egg with teeth like a beaver, and about Justine, the poodle with whom she shares him. She brags that Ethan is "an interior landscape designer," which is a big-deal title for watering, pruning and hanging houseplants in the big-fern bars and office buildings of San Francisco. He even has a contract with the God Is Not Dead Church across the street, Miss Kitty once explains, for they are a survivalist sect and plan to save all the flora of the earth after the new clear hollow cost.

Miss Kitty does not change her style a whisker

45

since I am a catling. She is seventeen now, white with black and orange knee socks.

"But what happens to your poor handsome face? It is full of scratches!"

I describe my encounter with Dolly Parrot and spell out my mission.

She begins her breathless reply. "Those poor little kittens! I don't believe a word of it, though, considering the source. You be careful of that floozie singer and don't go throwing yourself in her arms. Not that those kittens ever have a fighting chance anyway. After all, a child of Rex Boudoir has no legacy to brag about. None at all."

"Just the facts, Miss Kitty, just the facts."

"Always the tough guy, huh, Sue Slate? No time for old ladies or morals. Not that morals get Big Ole anyplace with his bible-thumping ways. And I don't mean just because he bites the litter. I know plenty. He is up to no good for months, ever since he leaves my Ethan and goes straight. He used to feed every hungry cat in the Alley including some not so hungry like your brother Dumpster who needs an extra meal like he needs a gift certificate to the flea market. I wish you would speak to Mr. Battle of the Bulge himself. What does he think, that he can work off his nip belly playing Rats and Mice?"

"Kitten —"

"Oh, flimdiddle. How often can I bend your handsome ear, Sue Slate?" She wiggles around, huffing a bit. "And what about that Computer Moll and her deviant bird that sounds like a Mack truck trying to brake all the way down Lombard every time it opens its horny little beak? What is she up to? That man is up and down her back stairs at all hours of the night. Not to mention Mr. Boudoir himself paying court to her under the arm of Mrs. Kling."

"What man?"

"The caped man I catch knocking on the Computer Moll's back door only once, but I am certain he is a regular. I am of the impression the Moll is normal like us, but I do not know what goes on behind closed doors. Something is funny there, I know that. The man's moustache is so bushy he can house whole families of homeless mousies. He is as skinny as a clothesline pole. But that's how this Alley goes lately, down, down, down. Why, everyone knows Bad Tuna Gat dispatches his runners all over the Mission to do his dirty work. Himself living so high off the hog he's bound to take a fall and soon. Not to mention the smell of dope everywhere Yellow Ethel goes. I sometimes wonder why she doesn't just float away. You can't blame this new generation for getting in so much trouble what with the likes of Rex and Bad Tuna running around. Why I remember —"

"The kittens."

"Yes, I am getting to the kittens, though why I must be your eyes and ears I don't know. If you don't gallivant about with your floozies you might see something once in a great while yourself. Ethan happens to schedule my annual visit with my physician that day and I therefore know nothing until I see Ms. Mimosa wailing outside Big Momma's door — I don't know *why* such a nice People takes that hussy in — wailing out there like she wants the world to think she suffers a personal loss. Are you certain *she* doesn't have something to do with the disappearance?"

47

The furs of my back bristle. "Do you see anyone near Big Ole's?" I ask.

Miss Kitty is quiet for the first time in seventeen years. I watch her face to make certain she thinks instead of snoozing. She is still a fine figure of a woman, balding pate and all. If I am as much of a swinger as she infers — but I am not. I am a one woman woman.

"There is one other visitor," she says. "Even bigger than Big Ole. Bald. All in white. There is yelling." She pauses. "You do not think *I* am going bald?" she asks, patting the thin fur under her ears. Then she rushes on. "He bends to stroke Bad Tuna. I think Bad Tuna is about to take his hand off, but instead he grovels, like this is the hand that feeds him. It is not any tough-as-snails Bad Tuna I ever see before."

"That's nails, Miss Kitty."

"Why does anykitty chew nails. Snails are tough enough."

We rub cheeks in goodbye and I admit that despite Miss Kitty's missing choppers, when she bats her eyes she is some heckova judy.

"You come on back, Sue Shamus!" she calls down the steps. "And next time not on business!"

I make my way slowly to the Cafe, licking my sore spots now that I am out of Miss Kitty's view. Miss Kitty lifts my spirits. Blue flowers like little stars light my way through the yard. I dig a fresh hole under the live oak for unmentionable purposes and contemplate the tree which twists around itself and dips to the ground before it lifts up to the sky.

Peacock Olley Cafe is dim inside and full of shady types. However I put on my best swagger and give the high sign to Olley. I am headed for the front window with a shot of nip and a milky chaser when Turtle Dove appears from the shadows and grabs my arm.

"Sue, Sue," she hisses.

I feel alarm at her haste, like maybe something is cracking on the case and Dumpster sends her.

"This one's guaranteed to slay you!" she says.

I give her a look which can kill large mosquitos at ten paces and try to move past her to discover what Humphrey uncovers since I tip him to the crimes.

But Turtle Dove is off and running and I figure I need her again some day. "This snail, see, she goes into a used-car lot and she is looking around."

I look over the bar and see that snails are the catch of the day at Olley's. No wonder they are on everykitty's mind.

"She is shopping for a car. Then she spots this 280Z and she says, *Wow, man, this is for me.* The snail goes up to the salesman and says, *I want to buy that, man — if you change the Z to an S.* The salesman, he says, *Well, lady, I don't think this is possible.* The snail tries to persuade him, but is unsuccessful. So she says, *Well, man, forget it.* But the salesman does not make a sale in many moons and she says, *Wait a sec. Let me consult with the authorities.* The boss he says, *What the hell, if it sells the car, change the darn Z to an S.* So the snail, she purchases the wheels with the S on, and she is all hopped up. She gets in and revs the engine and zooms out of there, peeling rubber all the way up the street. The salesman says to his boss, *Would you look at that S car go!*

"Cute," I tell Turtle Dove and run. Humphrey

has four clam juice cocktail empties lined up, so I know I need to talk fast. "The kittens," I say.

"There's some scuttlebutt that Rex Boudoir arranges this to shut up a wronged mama. And that he hires Bad Tuna to pull it off, but I smell some bigger fishes. Bad Tuna doesn't pull little jobs like that without some exterior purpose."

He takes a swig of the clam cocktail and licks his chops when it is gone. I oil his vocal chords with two bits for another cocktail.

"I suggest you put the screws on that torch singer. She walks around here biting off everycat's head these days. I hear the kittens resemble her too."

I stroll away feeling down on all fours. So much work and what can I show for it? Aches and pains, a noggin full of nasty suspicions that my gut does not go for and some very shaky leads.

I stalk a beetle along the strip, an activity which I find helps me to meditate. How can I ignore the slurs against my client? Miss Kitty and Humphrey have good heads on their shoulders; if they both mention her, it is up to me to knock the props out from under their doubts.

Chapter 8

"Oh, Big Girl," says Tallulah Mimosa with quite some alarm, "you look like you fight your way out of a niproom brawl. I hope it's not due to my case."

I am on her doorstep, fedora in hand, my parrot-inflicted injuries exposed to the light of day.

"And I'm not even there to dress your wounds! Come in, Sue Slate. Let me make it up to you somehow!"

I begin to suspect this parrot caper is worth the ordeal. You can just about knock me over with a feather — again — when Ms. Mimosa pulls me into her bed.

I am not loath to follow.

"Tell Tallulah all about it," she coos.

"Just a little trouble on the sleuthing circuit," I reply.

The judy insists on giving me a massage. I lie there and watch smudges of night blue shift in the white sky outside her window. With her gentle paws on me I am uncertain if it is heaven upon which I gaze, or if I am already moved in.

"Why your belly fur is just the color of ripe apricots!" she exclaims.

I move to cover this intimate patch.

"But it's beautiful! Oh, Sue Slate, you poor brave woman. I feel so responsible!"

My heart thuds with the nearness of her. I sense that she is about to lick my cheek. Her lovely black whiskers shine in the back-door light. Out in the city a firepopper explodes.

My voice is more hoarse than the caller at an all-day mouse auction when I say, "Tallulah."

"Sue," she says, sounding like she swallows fifty fishbones without chewing. I think The Big Smooch is about to occur.

Just then a whole string of firepoppers goes off right outside her door.

Tallulah leaps into the air screaming and lands again with every fur at attention. She looks at me with panic in those green eyes.

"Patches!" I hear from the other room. "Patches, are you all right in there?"

Tallulah whispers to me, "She can't rise fast

because of her arthritis. I've got to go to her. Goodbye."

I just stare at her. What gives with this grand bounce? Is it my Friskies breath? Then she leaves.

Dames, I think. I am too stunned to exit her love seat. In my head I play the pre-smooch over and over. I drift into a snooze with her perfume all around me.

When I awaken I catch vibes that something is amiss. For one, there is no Hot Paw boom-boom or other sound coming from Olley's Cafe. For two, I hear sobbing across the room in the dark.

"Ms. Tallulah?" I ask, as quiet as I can manage. Surely it is a national emergency that she is not at work tonight.

"Go away!" she sobs.

I do not want to blow it with this sweetpea. Why am I hanging around where I am unwanted?

Because I am a hard-boiled detective. I kick the stuffing out of a flea on my neck and think of Sherlock Holmes going for the truth.

I approach her. "I believe you have something to tell me, Ms. Mimosa."

"Go away!" she pleads.

I stop. No need to get Big Mom involved.

"Listen up, Powder Puff," I say, very quiet. "I apologize for catching a few Z's in your own sack, but it is not every day I am parrot-pecked half to death. I would not plan to wait around to talk to you, but since I am here and since you are here, why do we not just get down to business. I wish to know the facts, the whole facts and nothing but the facts."

She giggles.

"You are so darned cute, Sue Slate," says the

53

heretofore emotionally destroyed judy. "I don't know why you are suspicious of me, and Coddess knows my life is not a clean slate, so to speak. Yet I harm no one, only take care of myselves. I'll tell you my story if it serves to put your fears to rest."

"Thank you, Ms. Mimosa. This might greatly advance the progress of the case if I can cease to worry about you and go on to the real culprits."

She is smiling now. "Please call me Tallulah. And tell me why you suspect the woman who hires you to be what you call a culprit."

I clear my throat. I lick a speck off my saddle shoes. I cough.

"Do the kitnap victims," I ask, "are they yours and Mr. Boudoir's, Tallulah?" I am trying to listen like a professional, but my ears feel as full as two goldfish bowls.

She looks up at me in genuine horror. "How can you even think such a thing?"

"I must have answers in order to continue this investigation."

"I am never so insulted in all my lives."

"I know this is painful, Tallulah. You can take me off the case, but it is a personal matter now. I wish to wreak revenge on the criminal who perpetrates this skulduggery upon three innocent kittens and nothing can stop me no matter how it tears this Alley apart!"

"Then I have no choice but to tell you my story, Sue," Tallulah answers, wiping her eyes with a dear tawny paw.

Chapter 9

I was born, Tallulah began, *twenty-one years ago by the cat* calendar in a vineyard north of here. My parents settled in a large modern barn to work as tenant farmcats and to raise a family. Everything was lovely, sunny and lush, with mice for the taking and People who respected our work, fed us well and paid our health benefits. We were so proud of Daddy, who was a champion in the mouse rodeos held down by the river.

Our lives centered around those rodeos. We all trained for one thing or another, but Daddy was the star. He competed in the Tail Grab and his talent was unequaled. He could pin down even the scrawniest of mouse tails. In winter he excelled at Mud Tracking. In spring, the Leap and Truss, and in summer he'd win paws down at the Field Mousing Marathons. Every rodeo ended with an enormous barbecue and circle dance.

We had a lot of fun, but it wasn't always easy for Mom and Daddy. While he trained and trained to increase his winnings, Mom sold her famous Mousie Stew, which we kittens peddled. Of course, every year there was a new litter of kittens, but our parents managed to bring up every one of us to read and write, wear clean jumpsuits and use good table manners.

As a very young kitten my talent for singing was recognized and I studied with the greatest teacher in the county. With the discipline I learned from Daddy, I practiced till I dropped. Soon I was the star attraction at the fairs and rodeos with songs like "Stalking Through the Daisies." I would have been supremely happy if life had continued like this forever, but every blessing can turn into a curse. The two cats who were to change my life appeared within a month of each other.

The first was Slim Whiskers, a passing butch who set my heart on fire. She sat in the vineyard telling tales of her adventures in the railroad yards with the hobo cats. I followed every word; I could not take my eyes off her. She awoke in me a yearning to go to exotic places.

Needless to say, I threw myself at her as if she were the last train in the station. She was a gentle and thrilling lover. Though I was willing to follow

56

her to the ends of the earth, she was a loner and did not, she told me right at the start, "go a-travelin' with the burden of love in my bag."

And so it came to be that one day, two weeks after her arrival, I stood weeping at the gate, watching her sleek stripey head bob away toward San Francisco. I swore I'd follow her to the Golden City if I had to sell my soul. Little did I know that souls are dog-cheap where I was headed.

Mr. Jones Sump-Pump appeared the week after Slim Whiskers left. He was a rodeo scout who stank of leathery old stogies and afterbrush lotion. But he told me everything I wanted to hear about my future as a singer including a screen test with Disney and a club date at the Sandbox in Vegas. When he left he took me with him, reassuring my folks that he was the guardian angel to a bevy of up-and-coming stars and that he would protect me from charletans.

Not an hour from home, in a field, he explained what his fees were for being my agent. I left him with an ugly gash on his nose and minus an ear tip.

I ran as fast as I could and dropped exhausted behind some boxes. I fell into a deep slumber only to be awakened at dawn when the boxes around me began to jiggle. My hiding place was an open truck! My first urge was to leap off despite the truck's fast clip, but the memory of Mr. Jones Sump-Pump flooded back. I was so discouraged that I let fate drive me where it would.

As I watched, my old world flew by, blurring into the past. After a while the country was replaced by concrete, the farm houses by big buildings. Then I saw it, a sign for the Golden Gate Bridge. I was following Slim Whiskers after all!

The minute the truck stopped I jumped down. I had never seen so many People! I was in an alley and trucks were delivering all manner of things to a row of shops.

Famished, I made my way along the alley until I found a fish market. Case after case of glorious-smelling fishies paraded past me. I grabbed every piece of waste I could put my claws in.

It was the Mission District to which fate had led me. The first week I slept under stairs, on porches, in trucks, keeping an eye out for Slim. I never found her. Instead, the local toms found me. They drove me away from Mission Street with their terrible craving lusts.

So I wandered, hungry, cold and lonely through the damp streets. The farther uphill I roamed, the less room there seemed to be for cats. By Dolores Street I was convinced that my name was Git!

Then one night, staggering along 14th Street, I heard music. Even where I grew up Peacock Alley had a reputation for its night life. That I should stumble upon it seemed a sign.

I peered under the gate. The All-Edison Orchestra was playing ragtime. I longed to be up there scatting with them, but just inside the gate, toms loitered. Skinny and dirty I was still a well-shaped young woman and dared not pass.

Woogie took a solo. I liked his style. But what he played was a long way from a farm kitty's crowd pleasers. I knew at that moment that my free and easy days were over forever. Defeated, I curled up behind a trash can and dreamed all night of booing audiences.

In the morning a big woman came lumbering

toward me and lifted the trash can to put it on the street. I cowered in the shadow of the can.

"Oh, my," said Big Momma, "not another one."

I tried to get past her.

"Not so fast, my pretty one. I like your looks under all that matted fur. How would you like to get rid of your mites and your fleas and move on in with me?"

A home?

"Don't look so shocked. I'm a real patsy when it comes to strays. Half the cats in the neighborhood hit me up for meals, but, don't ask me why, you're special." She bent to pick me up. "Nothing to be scared of. You're going to like this."

And I did. She set out a huge dish of milk, bowls of dry and canned food, water and a bed. But best of all, she invited me, after a horrendous bath, onto her lap. It was wide and soft and warm, like Mom. Each time I woke there seemed to be another song playing. Song, I would think. Do I know this one or this one? Then I'd drop off to sleep again.

I came fully awake only when I felt Big Mom's teardrops falling down on me. I looked at her and she was staring at the picture box. The music playing then became my theme: "An Affair To Remember."

I spent many hours on her lap after that. Sometimes she would tell me tales of her days as a racehorse trainer. More often we watched TV and I learned a whole new repertoire of songs. Then I'd go up on the roof to practice. Finally I dared to approach Woogie. A charm fell over my life. Even though I found no one to replace Slim Whiskers, I was supremely happy.

Until Rex Boudoir began to pursue me.

59

Oh, Sue, I was lonely and desperate and foolish. I knew he could not be trusted, but I thought I could take care of myself around him. I didn't know what a cad he could be.

He would wine me and dine me out of respect for my art, he'd say. Later I learned that each meal was spiked with increasing amounts of nip soaked in an addictive substance. I began to yearn for our meetings, to tremble by the time he picked me up at my doorstep. I wondered if I could be falling in love with a man.

Then one night he apparently added a great deal more than usual of this substance to my meal and I became a prawn in his paws. He persuaded me to participate in a little practical joke he had planned — to take some of the stuffing out of Bad Tuna Gat and to teach him a lesson for all the harm he'd done.

Rex told me that Bad Tuna was running a courier operation. He has been hiring every down-and-out cat in the Alley to do the runs.

We went back to Big Mom's. It seemed like a great adventure to be prowling around San Francisco all night with a protector. Rex showed me his engraved silver derringer. We stopped somewhere for a snack. I can only assume it was as laced with drugs as dinner had been because after that I can't remember much. Just a lot of stairs and a huge white sign and the inside of a big building with pictures on the walls. It could have been a church, Sue. I don't know for certain, but something tells me it was the God Is Not Dead Church. Why would Rex bring me there? What could those hateful People have to do with the kittens?

Because that was the night the kittens disappeared.

When I came to in the morning I was back in my bed with no idea how I'd gotten there. I can't even tell you that I didn't have anything to do with the kittens' disappearance. Did Rex use me to lure them into Bad Tuna's net? I asked him.

"Don't worry about them," he told me, "and I won't let on about last night."

"What *about* last night?" I asked.

He tried to kiss me then. I wouldn't let him, of course.

"Come on, doll," he said. "Seal my lips with a kiss and no one will know about what you did in the dark of the night."

Now, Sue, I feel absolutely crazy. I don't know if he's trying to scare me into letting him seduce me, or if I really did something bad. Please don't think ill of me. This is the whole story, as far as I know it. Except for the green scarf.

I awoke with a lime green scarf around my neck which I've never seen before. I wore it during my performance the other night in hopes that someone would claim it, or at least recognize it, and help me to remember something more about that night.

Please, Sue Slate, find those babies. If I had anything to do with their abduction I am prepared to turn myself over to the Elders.

Chapter 10

Needless to say I am ready to give the rings off my tail to prove that Tallulah Mimosa is duped.

"Can you help me?" she asks.

I think of the Council of Elders and the punishment they mete out in the past to kitnappers. Banishment! I am not keen on losing this doll now that she is here. I look deep into her eyes. This time she does not run. She leans slowly toward yours truly and our noses touch. Indeed, it is the opposite of running away. She rests her sweet muzzle against mine. In the other room, Big Mom sniffles to romantic music from the picture box.

"Sure, Sweet Lips," I answer. "But we must review what you recall detail by detail. I need to be cognizant of every little thing, whether you think it is important or not."

"Whatever you say, Sue. I hold nothing back from you now."

"Nothing?" I ask, perhaps boldened by her proximity.

She looks deep into my eyes.

"Nothing, Sue. You are the hottest butch that has crossed my path since Slim Whiskers, and no fly-by-night if I guess correctly."

"You do indeed," I tell her. And then, out of mercy because of all she is going through, I propose that we have a little rest before we discuss these serious matters further. In this manner, I spend my first night with Tallulah Mimosa. I rate it a ten in terms of favorite methods of interrogation.

The next A.M. the Coddess of sunlight leaps over Tallulah's windowsill like a raging tigress. I figure this is a signal to begin my day's work pronto, so I nuzzle Tallulah's whiskers. I tell her I am off to run down the villains.

After breakfast at Levis's, which I get to eat because for once I beat Dumpster to the bowl, I decide to follow up on Tallulah's hunch about the God Is Not Dead Church. I also remember the hubbub outside the church lately, like they are recruiting for the Hundred Years' War.

I leave the sanctuary of Peacock Alley and cross the street to check out my goal. It is built more in the style of a fortress than a spiritual citadel. The walls are squared off. The narrow windows are designed for such objects as rifles in such sites as the Alamo, about which I study in Feline Herstory. Davie Crockitt is one of my early sheros. Around the roof is a notched wall. Into these notches can easily fit Onward soldiers and their cannons. Right now, pigeons hold down the fort.

My back fur rises. "It is only a church," I tell myself. Yet it lurks as dark and evil as a noonday shadow. Even Morty Mockingbird's songs at my back do not lift the pall. I walk around the edifice and find a back door propped open, as if the Rev. is due to return soon. I haul hiney over the threshold.

The building is stiller than a preying cat. I look in all the doors available to me, recalling that Miss Kitty's People Ethan does their plants. Indeed, this could be a full-time job, so many plants occupy these spaces.

Ah-ha! I say, then clap a paw over my mouth. One room has no plants and smells distinctly of a feline presence. I look in. It is a room filled with computers. As I creep inside the scent grows stronger. It is familiar, slightly rancid. Dumpster? No. He may be a slob, but he keeps himself clean. I tiptoe in, my claws sheathed for silence. Not a living soul in the room. There! Under that table, a carton. I approach it with extreme caution, one paw at a time, my ears extended at full capacity. The smell grows more potent, but even before I stand to look inside, I know it is an empty nest.

And then I know who uses this bed: it is Bad

Tuna Gat. His fur lies like a carpet across the rags that line the box. So this is another of his hideouts! A food dish on the other side of his bed tells me that he is welcome here. But why? And why then is he still a street cat, pretending to have no home but Big Ole's fire escape?

The room holds nothing else of interest. Just all those computers. What can they need so many for? I jump to one. It is the same as the Computer Moll's, right down to a small object with raised letters which reads M O U S E!

A sound issues from one machine like a hummingbird is trapped inside.

After some intense observation I spot something highly familiar. *HIV London* says the screen. *HIV Amsterdam.* Indeed, this is just like what I set eyes upon at the Moll's. How does it get here? Why does the church want such information? Does the Computer Moll know?

As my gray matter wearies due to frustration, I leave the computer room. A corridor leads into the church itself. The altar is alive with flourishing plants. The pews do not tempt me into napping. At the end of each of these affairs is an umbrella stand which puts me in mind more of a rifle rest.

As I explore I contemplate that glorious day when the Pope descends upon my fair town to speak a few pretty lines not far from here, at the famous Mission Dolores.

The night before the Pope's appearance, I must confess, all the cats in the District determine spontaneously to convert the Mission church into a giant litter box. The word on the Alley is that this Pope individual, with all his Missions, never sets up one Milky Kitchen to feed hungry cats, but instead uses his vast wealth on pomp and circumstance.

While the Pope speaks at Mission Dolores, the proud Mission District felines, peering in, note a distinct discomfort signaled by twitching human nostrils. In the sky, Glen Gull, leader of the local seagull movement whirls with his gang around and around the church, laughing like someone springs all the canned laughs at ABC.

In addition to this thoughtful contribution to the visit, we neglect our mouse-patrol and pigeon-control duties for some time prior. The Scavengers collect partially disintegrated objects to deposit under the pews. The Razzmatazzes spend the previous evening exhuming this and that from the Mission cemetery.

Needless to say, a good time is had by all and we do not expect a repeat visit from this Pope individual any time soon.

Meanwhile my wanderings take me to a storage area. Huge barrels are stenciled: DRINKING WATER and DEHYDRATED BEEF and EMERGENCY USE ONLY. Someone is planning a feast, I determine when I see shelves full of canned goods along the wall. I check for cat food, but evidently we are not invited.

Back in the church proper I note that the sun reaches the windows. Ah-ha! I say, but quiet as a mouse in hiding this time. For the windows look not unlike large pictures. Can this be what Tallulah recalls? Stained glass church windows?

I make my retreat and arrive at Levis's in time to

raid the countertop. I am hungry enough to steal the dog's dinner. He leaves a tin of sardine oil and the rind from some Camembert. I dip the rind in the oil and imbibe a most luxurious repast. Then I settle in my bed and drift into a well-deserved nap while I relish the aging mix of flavors on my palate.

I am awakened when Dumpster raids a cabinet and I hear the familiar sound of Friskies raining on linoleum. I amble out to watch this routine.

"What's that on your ruff, bro'?" I ask to make conversation. "Last night's minnow salad?"

Turtle Dove sidles up to me, perhaps to prevent a confrontation. "Listen, Sue, this is dishious. A limp-wristed lily says to her hunk, honey I wish to be frank with you tonight. Naw, says the hunk, *I'm* Frank tonight. You were Frank *last* night! You get it?" She cackles like Doll Parrot over this stale jest.

When Dumpster comes up for air I accost him.

"If you are looking for a racket, Dumpster, you can stake out the Computer Moll's pad. Something smells fishy-like around computers here and I wish to know if someone is heisting her data. I find the same gibberish over at the God Is Not Dead."

Turtle Dove suggests, "Maybe *she* is heisting *their* data. Why else would she spend all her time at the computer and have all those strange visitors?"

I mull this over as prior to now I simply consider anyone who takes in a beast as vile as Dolly Parrot must be on the side of the angels. "Of course I consider this," I tell Dove. "Why do you think I call for a stake-out? I must resolve the discrepancy."

"Always willing to accommodate you, Sis, on a steak-out."

"I'll bring the A-1 Sauce!" says Turtle Dove.

I ignore her. "Do not forget what Mom always says," I remind Dumpster.

"Yeah. Keep your tail covered."

Chapter 11

The Fourth of July is upon me. I am apprised of this fact as I attempt to grab a couple of extra winks in the A.M. Bang, pow, pop. I am grinched out, but duty calls like a nagging bluejay.

With my brother on the job, I am free to persist in my investigations. Procedure at this point calls for continued interrogation of witnesses. Who should come to mind but my own cousin Tailspin, a half-Siamese with a trendy brown moustache and a physique worthy of Catlas. I spot him posing on a ledge between two pots of blazing red begonias.

"Whoa there, you low-life gumshoe," he says. He wears a cowboy outfit today: a vinyl collar decorated with red horseshoes. Tailspin is a vinyl queen. "Where you'all goin in such an all-fire rush, Cuz?"

"Beating the bushes for you." I explain my business posthaste. He often acts as Dumpster's fourth leg on stakeouts when they are cruising buddies. Prior, that is, to the time Dumpster and Cooky became steady beaus due to the dangers posed by Feline Leukemia Virus.

He ripples his tan fur and stretches. "Just what's this dish you seek worth to you, Cuz?"

"What do you have, Tailspin?"

He flicks his whiskers. "I have facts on my facts, honey. I'm in and out of the Computer Moll's all the time with Yellow Ethel."

"Are you into feathers too?"

"Ugh. Filthy things. Ethel bribes the bird with palm reefers to keep her put. The Moll has the most gorgeous vinyl couch. I spend hours on it." He sprawls along the ledge like it is a sofa. "Ouch!" He tugs at a sliver of wood which threatens his posterior. "I simply cannot abide these natural materials. So imperfect."

"Ever see this before, Tailspin?" I show him the rhinestone I pick up off the Computer Moll's rug.

He examines it carefully. "It's not one of mine. First of all, I'm not missing any; second, it's ostentatious. Why not try Rex Boudoir? He wears rocks the size of a St. Bernard's foot."

"Okay, then. Spill it."

"Ahem."

"Name your price."

70

"I'm not greedy, Marshall Slate, but there is this gorgeous burgundy naugahyde collar —"

I hand him some chicken feed. He moves closer to me and speaks in a purr.

"A People in a cape and spectacles. This is the Computer Moll's most frequent visitor."

"Bushy moustache?"

"How do you know?"

"What do they do?"

"Not much. The Moll pokes at the computer and gives Cape-O enough paper to carpet Castro Street. Sometimes they're very excited about what this computer says and sometimes they're very sad. They talk a lot about beating the Grim Reaper. I never see him, though."

"Do you ever see a big hairless People all in white?"

Tailspin contemplates his well-manicured claws for a minute. "No. Maybe he's the Grim Reaper?"

I look at him. Can he be serious? "Perhaps," I answer, "metaphorically speaking."

As I walk away he evens the score. "Hey, Cuz! Who does the mermaid make eyes at?"

I am caught by surprise. "Who"

"All the ocean swells!"

His laughter follows me. Last year the fad is yo-yos, this year soft corn.

It is high noon. Hot puffs of breeze carry the sun. I jump a fence and make a quick snack of the moist grass that grows between the roses. Then I climb to the roof of an Alley edifice. The tar is warm and gives under my pads. I note some activity in a far corner. With the intent of loud courtesy I clear my

71

throat. Two figures slink up from a four o'clock shadow.

Leonora puts on her Professional Feline Potential Movement smile. "You could warn us."

"You neglect to send me your makeout schedule this week," I counter.

Yellow Ethel is in a languorous position. "Do not be so uptight, Leo, baby," she instructs her elder. She is scruffy, skinnier than ever and her eyes run. I do not seek it, but Ethel always evinces unwanted passions for this exotic private eye.

She snaps her juicy-fish gum at me. "Bet you get to see a lot of the world," she says with a wiggle in the vicinity of her tail.

I check her paramour for jealous noises. However, her Movement teaches alpha waves, not upset feelings. I introduce the business at paw. "It comes to my attention that you occasionally habituate the porch of the Computer Moll."

"What's it to you?" Ethel says, looking away.

"As I understand you are also under the tutelage, shall we call it, of one Bad Tuna Gat. I am interested to know if he assigns you to this domicile."

Leonora interjects, "She's *not* associated with that cretin any more."

"What are you, my mother?" spits Yellow Ethel. I am curious what brings a type like calm Leonora to fall for such a spitfire. Maybe she is of the rescuing sort.

"Is it true what I hear about Mr. Tuna diversifying his services into gathering and disovulating information?"

Ethel gets a crafty glint in her eyes. She rolls them toward Leonora, then shuffles my way, sniffling.

She has a soaked-nip habit or my name is not Sue Slate, Private Eye.

"Everybody around here knows Bad Tuna keeps a flock of stool pigeons on the roof. Always has."

I get tough with her. "You know this is not what I refer to."

"I know nothing." She turns tail and walks away. I notice her hygiene can use improvement.

"I am investigating the kitnapping," I say.

She stops, swings her head around. "Those three little kittens that are lifted?"

Leonora pipes up. "What do you know about them, Ethel?"

"Not a darned thing."

I give Leonora my seven megaton nuke look.

"What about," I ask Ethel, "a certain flurry of activity having to do with computers?"

"Oh, that!" says Ethel with a guilty squeak. "You mean the computer disk Bad Tuna loses last week? What a joke. After all his years filling contracts and dealing dope, one little thing like that causes such a ruckus. And he never sees the thing! It's hijacked before it's turned over to him with the rest." She looks at Leonora from the corner of her eye. "This is what I get on the grapevine."

A *likely story*, I think.

"Since when does Bad Tuna deal in computer disks?"

Leonora drapes her arm across Ethel's shoulders. "What are you up to, Sue Slate?" she asks. "My protege is through with Peacock Alley crime. She means no one harm."

"No one," I say with a growl, "but the kittens in the schoolyard panting for a fix." Ethel cringes under

73

her caretaker's arm. "No one, but their mothers who do not know why they steal, cheat and lie. No one but herself, for not getting clean and sober. No one."

"That is the past, Sue Slate," says Leonora. "Ethel runs with the wrong crowd back then. Our encounter groups work wonders with her since!"

I give one last look at Ethel, then go back over the wall. Maybe the kid straightens up eventually, but all the Movements in the city cannot do it for her. Meanwhile, I decide to let her stew in her own filthy-type conscience.

Chapter 12

It is high time, I decide, to shoot some questions at Rex Boudoir.

From the top of Leonora's fire escape I survey his windows. His People, Mrs. Kling, moves like a wind-up toy much in need of oiling. Someone paints a smile on her mouth, but forgets to take the nasties out of her eyes. Yet she has a rep for finding homes for strays, so I deduce she cannot be all bad.

When I arrive at the window, she is in the kitchen banging pots and pans and stirring batter in a bowl like it is her worst enemy. Her feline philanderer is in a sheepskin-lined basket big enough to house him and all his cast-off progeny.

I lower my hat to cover a laugh. This piss-elegant stud, with every coppery fur in place, has his head between his legs and is licking his bottom clean, smacking his chops every few strokes.

I clear my throat. He looks up and gets a shit-eating grin on his face. "Well, well, it's our ogler-for-hire. Want a treat?" he asks.

"Close those scrawny clodhoppers, you walking ego."

"Why, Slate? You need some lessons on how to do it."

"I have no interest in dragging schoolgirls behind bushes, Boudoir."

He splashes on some Old Mice After Lick Lotion.

"I do have earnest interest in identifying the malefactor in the Case of the Kitnapped Kittens."

"What makes you think it's one of us, Miz Diesel-of-the-Year? With all you rough and tumble dykes around I'm surprised there isn't more bloodshed in your lovers' spats."

The cat's intellect is not large enough to run a shoeshine operation.

"You prowl the Alley nights. What do you see of this event?"

"Sorry, dog-face. You're barking up the wrong tree. I'm a party man, remember? I see no evil, hear no evil, only do evil."

I study his collar, but cannot discern if he is missing some rocks as the usual flotsam and jetsam are gathered around his magnet. I wonder what it takes to pry information from this midget-mind.

"All I ever see is dolls under the moonlight, Slate.

However, if it makes your life complete, I can fling your way any dirt I pick up — for a price."

Something shakes my leaves. I am certain Rex is lying, but I do not know why. He kicks metal off his collar. Indeed, a gap in his rhinestones appears. I gauge its size. It is about right for the glitter I pull out of the rug.

"What about Big Ole? Spend much time with him, Rex?" I ask to distract him as I roam around the room, sniffing out what disturbs me. I am certain that there is something right before my nose that I am not registering. The room is as neat as a brothel at twilight. However, all I can smell is Mrs. Kling's perfume.

"That old pansy? I have no business with his kind."

I make for the couch.

"Or with Bad Tuna Gat?"

Rex sniffs and sticks his aristocratic nose in the air. "Miz Slate," he says. His voice sounds choked. "It's one thing to barge in here uninvited, but if you are planning to take a snooze you'd better give it another think."

I surmount the couch and then I see it. A filmy lime green scarf stuffed behind the cushions. Is this not the one Tallulah describes? The one that just appeared on her neck the morning after the kitnapping? Yes, the scent of Roemance is all over it.

This wises me up no end. Humphrey warns me. Miss Kitty warns me. But I fall for Mimosa's line and wish in all innocence to jump on her bones. The lying, double-crossing —

"Rexy!" It is Mrs. Kling like a leaning tower of KalKan in the kitchen doorway. Her voice is like a

77

claw on a blackboard. "You've brought home a new playmate, I see. Not nearly as pretty as that calico who's always up here."

At this Rex packs up his manners like they just lose a hundred points on the hog belly market. He rushes me, yowling like I am the heathens come to desecrate his temple.

"Vamoose, Slate. The old bag abhors you lowlife strays."

I am backed into the corner of his sullied love seat, holding Tallulah Mimosa's scarf in front of me. "What is *this*, Casanova? Does Tallulah come to you of her own free will?"

He growls in a manner foreign to his public persona. "Get out, you slimy snoop."

Mrs. Kling springs into the room now, a broom at her chest like a Uzi.

I grab the scarf in my teeth and hot-foot it to the window before this sweet-big-old-lady type completely turns into a wolfperson.

"Vermin!" she yells as we run around the room, toes to heels. "Scum! How dare you molest my bee-oo-tiful Rex! I will not have cat fights in my living room! Rex has a pedigree longer than your tail!"

I pause once I am out the window and turn. Mrs. Kling picks up Rex who blasts out a purr that can melt a snowcat.

Chapter 13

It is nearing the hour for my evening repast. I am
filled with yearning for nothing but to reach Casa
Levis before Dumpster hogs all the chow. However,
my eyes light upon some commotion up at Big Ole's
pad and I resign myself to tightening my belt a notch
or three.

From the pickup in firepopper business, Fourth of
July is rattling down the street like a trolley sans
brakes. Even the chorus birds are excited. The leaves
of their rehearsal tree rustle till I think the branches
dance.

A stern-looking Alice Blue Gown greets me at the scene of the crime. *"Scat!"* he roars.

I begin to feel rejected.

"Let it be," says a man inside. "There's cat fur all over the deceased's apartment, and a cat bed out on the fire escape, but the neighbors say he didn't have a pet." He comes for me and looks me eyeball to eyeball. "I wish you could talk, pussycat. I have a few questions for you."

Now it is not that I am against cooperating with the gendarmes. Or that I am not anxious to get to the bottom of our mutual dilemma. But I have a feeling that if I let on my comprehension of his every word, I would be transported to a kitty laboratory for research quicker than you can say codcakes. Goodbye long days of lolling in the sun. Goodbye sleuthing practice. Goodbye lullabies from Peacock Olley Cafe. Goodbye to the green shimmery scarf I tie around my neck in order not to lose it.

The People go through Big Ole's place making a mess. I watch, settling on the window ledge to clean myself. Out of the corner of my eye, though, I notice that Bad Tuna Gat lies in the back hallway, his cheeks resting against one of Big Ole's uniforms. This is not outside last time I am here.

He looks at the uniform like it is a beloved. Then he begins to lick it. The next thing I know, he kneads it with his front paws. This is not Bad Tuna I ever see, mooning over some People's dirty clothing. Yet everykitty loves, and perhaps Big Ole is the only one to show he cares since Bad Tuna's mom dies. I can just barely hear a few of his words.

". . . all my fault . . . Big Friend . . . gone like Ma . . ."

I crane my neck a little too far. He spots me, jumps up, kicks at the uniform like he uses it for elimination purposes, and stalks down the steps.

"What is it with the rag around its neck?" queries Blue Gown.

I snap to attention. The plainclothes fuzz looks at me and the scarf such a very long time that I begin to back toward the door.

I move too slowly.

A meatloaf hand clamps around the scruff of my neck and I am airborne. Without a 'chute.

He dangles me in front of his face. Just out of reach of my claws. "Where did you pick up this bit of scarf, pussy?"

I spit in his eye.

He crushes me to his chest with the other meatloaf. I puncture it with my fangs. Well, I try. It does not taste anything like the meal I aspire to anyway.

"Now, now, naughty puddy," he says. "Calm down or I'll get the men in the puddy van to pick you up for assaulting an officer of the law."

I determine that the best defense right now is no offense. He sets me on the couch and I go limp. He removes said scarf from my neck. Rag indeed. As if Tallulah would wear rags. I watch the push-out type window swing in the breeze. The sun is on the wane and beckons me to follow. I force my back fur to lie at ease.

"There, there now," the copper says. "You were just frightened. Animals like me."

The Blue Gown put in his two cents. "Too bad there's no collar on it. We could trace the owner."

"No need, no need," answers meatloaf-hand.

"Anyone in the neighborhood can tell us where this ferocious little puddy lives." I roll onto my back with an endearing purr.

Uniform snickers at his boss. "I bet *all* the girls roll over for you just like this one."

I force my claws to sit tight in their sheaths while I noodle out a plan. A professional like myself concentrates on the bottom line. Like getting out of this alive. Yet images of Bad Tuna Gat sounding so woeful distracts me.

He digs in his pocket and produces another piece of green material just like Tallulah's.

Holy dog turds, I almost say.

"The other half," he explains. I see for the first time that Tallulah's scarf indeed has a ragged edge.

"I found this, puddy, balled up in the victim's hand. It made me wonder if the murderer might be a woman. And if you can lead me to her."

Ah-ha! I think. *But what woman?*

"How could a woman overpower a big guy like that?" asks Blue Gown.

"Maybe she was someone he trusted. Remember, we don't know the exact cause of death yet, only that his skull was bashed in. And that tiny puncture wound. The lab is checking on hypo use. Of course, he's a nurse. He could have stuck it in himself."

I do not know what makes me feel worse at this juncture in time, being a helpless feline on her back, or experiencing heart throbs for Tallulah Mimosa, the wearer of the clue. I feel despondency approach like a stalking tick. Life is not worth one fishbone. *Is* she haunch-deep in this? How can I itch for a wicked woman?

Why does she shine me on if she's guilty of

something? To prove her innocence? Is her life story all lies?

It is imperative that I exfiltrate myselves.

The coppers poke around the rooms. I lower my legs, sink my back claws deep into the couch and blast off, wresting the scarf from meatloaf on my way.

"The puddy — I mean the cat!" yells Blue Gown.

Meatloaf's fingers close around my tail as I hit the windowsill.

Chapter 14

Disengaging my nether extremity from the long arm of the law is a struggle, but this I accomplish and flee into the twilight crowds gathering in Peacock Alley.

Hot Paws warms up with a Spanish beat and Woogie teases the crowd with brassy notes. Before I can catch my breath from my escapade, Tallulah swings into a hot marimba on stage while the Birdy chorus line whirls behind her.

My stomach feels like the birdies dance inside it. The noise, the crowd's restlessness — I sense something amiss. I scan the faces. Bad Tuna shouts over Tallulah's song to his syncophant, Roary, who roars with laughter at every joke. Is it really Bad Tuna I observe carrying on at Big Ole's?

Rex gloms Tallulah from the bar, looking like the cat about to swallow the canary. His rhinestones twinkle; the gap on his collar laughs at me for not knowing how to pull this case together. Oh, to poke Rex in the snout — but I do not do strong-paw work.

Dumpster swings himself up beside me, looking fresh from his surveillance.

I whisper, "What'd you smoke out?"

Turtle Dove arrives, breathless, and hugs me. I bat her away.

Dumpster looks as serious as a hungry bumblebee. "There is something going on in Peacock Alley, Sis. Too much traffic up and down the back stairs, People and cats. Up at Big Ole's place the cops are throwing out the dragnet for a certain jock stripey. They talking about you?"

"Just what I need," I reply. I do not have time to go into hiding. Tallulah's neck is in the noose.

"Tell her about God Is Not Dead," Turtle Dove pipes.

"Ever since the kitnapping these fiends wear a trail from the church to the Computer Moll's. And there's always some scruffy guttercat sleeping on her fire escape — keeping an eye peeled, if you catch my drift. This Cape-O guy's there half the night from what I hear."

Turtle Dove leans in front of me and talks fast. "Why should you not ever court a john in the garden? Listen! Because the corn has ears, the potatoes have eyes and the beans talk!"

Dumpster glares at her.

"What do the Moll and Cape-O do in there?"

"Play with that computer business."

"What a silly bore," says Turtle Dove.

"Is this all you have?" I ask.

"No, Sis. I know who Cape-O is."

"Who?"

"Levis."

"Our Levis?"

"Our Levis. I peg him when Ethan and his poodle come to the Computer Moll's door. Levis takes off that cape and that big hat for once. I don't know why the disguise, unless the Moll doesn't want anyone thinking she's got a male visitor —"

Can everyone I trust be turning on me?

"He has a big fight with Ethan," says my brother. "Something about not wanting him to come barging in. I can't make head or tails of it."

"What's the Computer Moll doing through all this?"

"Madly working at her computer, what else?"

On stage, Tallulah breaks. The hubbub grows around us. "We are on the trail of something that has to do with computers, something that has to do with scientists, something about the church Big Ole belonged to, and something that Bad Tuna has his paw in. It is like a spider's web. Maybe this cure business is at the center of it all. Thanks for the lowdown, Dump."

"Rain de toot, Sis." He licks his white bucks. "There's one more thing. I hear this songbird of yours knows a lot more than's good for her."

I growl at him. "This is not true."

86

"And I hear you are spending a lot of time with her."

"Not nearly enough, you stomach-on-feet." Then I take a deep breath, hoping what I say is true. "Listen, give credit where credit is Sue. And you keep this under your ears. Tallulah is all gummed up in the spider web, but only because Rex is threatening to frame her if she does not fork over her favors. She knows nothing, you understand? Nothing. I only tell you this so you are not distracted in your pursuit of the real criminals."

"You want I should lean on this Boudoir character?" He picks his teeth with a long sharp claw.

Mmm. I am tempted to scare the waves out of Rex's coat, but decide it is best not to let on that we suspicion a thing.

"No. Your next assignment is to discern the destination of Bad Tuna's hired help. He is operating a courier operation. What does he relay?"

Dumpster rises. "Aw revore, Sis."

"Time for one more!" cries Turtle Dove. "Did you hear the one —"

Just then comes the sound of a loud crack. A firepopper up on stage? I see Tallulah fall. The crowd yowls and surges forward. I start to race to her side, but cannot tear my way through the cats crazed with horror. Woogie is with her, I see, and little Hot Paws. Olley is shouting the crowd back. Three members of the All-Edison Electric Orchestra play Coddess Save the Elders.

What if Tallulah is no more? How can I finally find the love of my life only to lose her?

What is done is done. She is in good paws, I tell myself. I survey the rooftops. A light-colored cat disappears behind a ledge. My duty is clear. I shag after the figure with the swiftness of revenge.

Chapter 15

Just as I gain the rooftop, the cat disappears over the other side. Even as I give chase, I am aware of the shouts still rising from Peacock Alley, and the muffled sounds of firepoppers under a helmet of fog.

Paws hit a tin rooftop below me. I scramble after the scalawag over walls and through fences. I think she is aimed at the God Is Not Dead like everyone else these days, but no, she veers off like she is changing her mind in mid-sidewalk, and I get a good look at her as she runs under the lit cross.

Cream-colored, with brown and copper patches. Probably a great grandchild of Rex's.

I pursue said beast down 14th Street like a greyhound addicted to rabbits. Fireworks light up the fog and inspire a pace more swift than a mouse stealing from a cat food bowl. She streaks across Valencia, past the armory, and before I know it, we are on Mission Street, alien turf.

This is for the birds. We dash under a throng of People spinning sparklers, past street musicians beating drums, under neon signs: DOC'S CLOCKS, COCKTAIL TIME.

This cat is slick. She darts into an open doorway; I follow. Before me is a forest of table legs. The place is full of spicy smells. I lose sight of her, then hear a shriek and a crash. Big round trays roll past me. There are tortillas and ice cubes all over the floor. My brakes fail as I slide through the mess and land splat against a white pant leg. I know right away I am in big trouble and leap up, trying to shake the squashed beans from my back feet.

Ah hah! The villain sneaks a glance under the swinging kitchen doors. I leap, but am vanquished by an ice cube. Not for long. Through great ingenuity, I land on a gaggle of cubes and sled my way under the doors only to be stopped by the villain herself, yowling on impact. She leaps to a countertop, lands on a plate and flips back to the floor. The cooks holler like World War Three just breaks out in their kitchen.

She jumps to a metal table and skids into a bowl of red sauce. Indeed, she emerges from the bowl like some monster of the deep Red Sea.

"Yipes!" I cannot help but exclaim.

She scoots away from me and straddles a bowl of onions in order to fling them at me with her back feet. Never having been maced before, I am soon in tears, too blind to see. When my eyes clear, the scoundrel is vamoosed and a red-faced People in white clothing bears down on me, wielding a knife which quite definitely does not serrate grapefruit for a living.

I head for the back door. It is closed. The man lunges. I sidestep him.

A voice shouts, "Hey, man! Don't make another mess for me to clean up!"

The door opens. I am gone.

In the back alley, I catch my breath. I am not one to wallow in self-pity, but I dive in with my fur on this time. Here I am, all alone in a neighborhood I do not know, reeking of onion, engaged in guerilla warfare in a holiday combat zone: bang! pow! pop!

There is a trail of red sauce leading out of the alley.

I spot her crossing Mission Street at a great velocity, dodging honking cars, People on the sidewalks, barking dogs. A fried-chicken shack emits delectable whiffs and I nearly faint, except fainting can ruin my image.

Without warning she dips under a metal gate. I am on her heels. Sweet alyssum grows all over, swallowing her up. Only by the weeds' movement can I follow and then, the weeds go still.

Is she waiting to ambush me? Signaling a local gang for help? A cricket belches. I stay as still as if I am mousing. A flash in the sky, another, explosions. Of all times to be in hot pursuit of a sniper, on the Fourth of July.

I sniff, think I smell something, but the breeze takes it. I pick it up, follow it again, it shifts.

My good senses determine this to be a useless exercise. I climb a pile of bricks. Fireworks go off. I hit the dirt. My nerves are ragged.

I spy out a beat-up old tom of a building. The windows at ground level are all smashed in. Can my prey be inside? Should I return to Peacock Alley for reinforcements? No time. No time!

I creep forward and round a clump of grass to reconnoiter. And pense. Can I ever get home to assess for myself how much damage this punk causes Tallulah? Is Tallulah alive? Does she think I am running from her trouble? Who can assassinate such a fine woman?

I step to the first window. No sound from within. Then I see lights and I duck. Are there People in the guts of the old tom building? I peer over the hill, careful of glass shards, of being sighted, of making a sound.

Suddenly I realize where the lights are coming from!

Chapter 16

Foul language courses off my tongue. The lights are *not* inside. As a matter of fact, nothing is inside. Said lights issue from the next structure.

The would-be assassin is most probably vamoosed through my own self-pity and cowardice. For all I know, she is skulking along the Embarcadero right now.

My extraordinary homing instinct directs me back to the Alley from Mission Street. At least I am not harmed and can continue the business of rescuing

Tallulah Mimosa. Woogie stands guard outside Big Mom's window.

"How is she?" I whisper.

He grins his big sad sloppy grin and points the way to the kitchen. I feel his glowing yellow eyes on me all the way, probably wishing Tallulah asks for him in her dying moments. Poor Woogie.

Then I realize something is amiss. I stop and look back at Woogie with no little astonishment. Through the air wafts a scent far from deathly.

Woogie shrugs his hairy shoulders as if to say, *Don't look at me. I only love her.* Then he speaks in his growly resigned voice. "She's all yours, Sue Slate, Private Eye." He pauses on the windowsill. "Darn it," he finishes.

The pretty in the kitchen is a sight for a weary crimebuster's eyes. I forget myself and take her into my arms. Fireworks splash through the night sky.

"You are a fine furry moll," I say.

Tallulah throws back her head and laughs with a low purring sound. I bury my face in her silken white ruff. "There is no sign of a bullet at all," she tells me. "Just this."

She shows me a lump on her head where she is beaned by a small object.

"But how —"

"We think the sniper just waits for a fire popper to explode, then hurls this." In her paw is a small sharp stone. "We used to do this all the time as kids on the farm to scare the dogs away. It is the oldest trick in the world."

"But why —"

"Woogie thinks someone's trying to frighten me."

She hugs me to her again. "I'm too happy to be alive to feel any fear tonight, Sue Slate. My only thought through the whole ordeal is this: how can I die now that I find you?"

I hold her tighter than a tree limb in a windstorm. Little by little we begin to move and I realize Tallulah is waltzing me around, humming our song. Around and around we go until yours truly stumbles from dizziness.

"I'm sorry!" cries Tallulah.

"No, no. It is my fault. I do not imbibe a morsel of nourishment since noon and it is now the next day!"

Five minutes later I pop the top off some Chateau Nova Scotia, '76, a bubbly cod liver oil with an excellent bouquet. Tallulah serves a cold casserole of beef liver à la goat cheese with a crust of pulverized Pounce pellets. For dessert there is a strong runny Brie which she smears across my paw for us both to lick.

"So you can cook too," I conclude, stifling a small burp.

Over the last of the bubbly I recount my Mission Street adventure.

Tallulah listens with wide batting eyes and gives me a nuzzle for my bravery. "Also," she says, "I remember something tonight."

"A clue?"

"I think so. It happens when I'm hit. As I lie onstage I hear a conversation again in my mind. One voice belongs to Big Ole."

"Then you *are* on the scene the night of the kitnap. Who is the other voice?"

She shakes her head. "I cannot place it. But she says —"

"*She?*"

"I think so, though I do not swear to it before a courtyard of Elders. It is high-pitched, but bellowing, and makes my ears twitch. She tells Big Ole that he can't back out now. That he must help to rid the city, the world, of these elements."

"What elements?"

"Be patient, my love. Big Ole shouts, *I won't do something like that! I'm into spreading the Lord's word, not rattling swords!* Then the awful voice yells, *Babel is at our door! The Lord is coming, but we must cleanse the world to prepare for Him!*"

Tallulah shudders. I place an arm about her shoulders.

"Big Ole booms out, *Who appoints you the Lord's redeemer? Stop or I'll go to the authorities!*"

"Ah-ha! A motive."

"The other voice says, *It's gone too far for that, you Benedict Arnold! We cannot turn our backs on the Company now!*"

"What company? In cahoots with the God Is Not Dead?"

"This is when the doc reaches me onstage. I come out of my daze and the voices stop. Only —"

"Only what?"

"There's something about your trip to Mission Street. Something about the building you describe. I can see myself in such a building. Recently, though I am unaware of being away from here at all. Can this be where Rex takes me? I remember going up and up and up. And then white, a lot of white."

"White inside, a mess outside. This sounds like a

perfect hiding place for some kind of operation. But what? And what lady dares to order Big Ole around? The coppers think it is a lady who murders Big Ole."

"The voice is familiar, Sue, like sour milk. And a heavy perfume." She bends her head. "This is all I can recall. I am sorry."

I touch her paw. "You give me more than I ever expect, Tallulah."

She looks up at me, as if to see if my meaning is double-edged.

I flick two whiskers to tell her it is. "You must be exhausted."

"No, Sue Slate. I am exhilarated. By you."

Now is the moment, I tell myself. She is mine for the taking. I want her more than any woman I ever want before. But I am a loner, a private eye. Look at my lost love Trixie. I have no right to lay claim on a woman I cannot be there for. Still . . . "Tallulah —"

"Yes, Sue?" she answers, short of breath.

"I — I —" I stop, straighten my shoulders. "I need to strike while the fire is hot. Can you return to Mission Street with me tonight?"

Chapter 17

Out the window we go into the dark mysterious alleyways of San Francisco. The city sounds not unlike a hundred thousand sleepers breathing. The pigeons snore: coo-kitty-coo. Eucalyptus is a perfume everywhere. It is so late even the God-Is-Not-Dead sign is doused.

"Are you certain you wish to accompany me?" I ask Tallulah. "This may be a dangerous mission."

Her eyes are as golden as the squares of windows wherein lovers lie awake by candlelight. Her hands fumble at the lime green scarf I return to her and which she wears like a reminder of her folly. "Yes, Tiger," she responds. My heart flutters. The lights of the Bay Bridge twinkle beyond her. "I wish to bring this kitnapper to justice and to find the poor little souls. But also, I wish to be your helpmate, Sue Slate. I love you for your honorableness, your nobility, your caring and your gentleness."

I wish for a video of this moment to cherish as long as I live. Unfortunately, I am not certain that this is likely to be a long time due to the circumstances facing me. However, I cannot back out at this late date. Better to die a heroine in Tallulah's eyes than to linger on earth without her respect.

"You are a brave companion, Ms. Mimosa," I proclaim. "Come. I feel it is advisable at this juncture to notify my brother of our whereabouts in case we do not return in a reasonable amount of time."

We go to Levis's, but no Dumpster. We try the back of Peacock Olley's and a few other hangouts, to no avail. Then I remember Darlin'. Levis tells him earlier that he expects to be out late and this means that Darlin' is at his own place. Dumpster may be tending him.

"Dumpster!" I call softly through a window, keeping low in order that Tallulah does not see inside. I am certain he would prefer as much as I that no one know about his nursey-nursey life.

"It is two o'clock in the A.M.!" he growls, but appears in the window, straightening his stripey pajamas.

"Do I interrupt something?" I ask.

"Coddess, do I deserve a rest. I sleep all day until I am exhausted. I need this tonight like I need another stripe."

He does indeed sound disturbed.

"You got to help me, Sis." His voice quavers. "Darlin' is gone. The front door is open and the pad is a mess. He even leaves Esmeralda behind."

"Esmeralda?" asks Tallulah.

"His teddy bear. She is an offensive green," I explain before I realize that I let the dog out of the bag. How do I know Darlin's sleeping habits unless I too play nursey-nursey?

Dumpster is looking at me funny.

"Is there sign of a struggle?" I ask quickly.

"Nothing is disturbed, except his medicine which is disappeared."

"Then," suggests Tallulah, "maybe he leaves on vacation, or goes to the hospital, and a burglar comes by."

Dumpster squints at me, kicking a cowlick into place.

"You can talk freely in front of her," I tell him.

He leads us into Darlin's bathroom. Dumpster learns his lessons well: his powers of observation begin to approach normal. There is a wadded piece of paper stuffed into the sink drain.

"I replace it there in case someone looks for it."

I unroll the note. Something bothers me about it right out of the chute.

Lover, Just discovered where Ricky and Tom have disappeared to. Don't worry. This is for the best. If it shouldn't work I've lost nothing. Tried to call you. No answer."

We look at one another.

"Darlin' has beautiful penmanship. I wonder why he doesn't use it?" says Turtle Dove, looking over my shoulder.

100

Just then the box by the telephone whirs. Darlin's voice comes on, repeating the words it always says. Then a buzz and Darlin' again, but this time whispery and scared. "Lover, are you there? I've made a big mistake. They're not watching — I grabbed the phone. This isn't a clinic, it's a — They're coming! Mish —"

The receiver slams.

"This smells fishy, right?" asks Dumpster.

"To the high heavens," Tallulah agrees. "What does he mean by *mish?*"

"A name?" Turtle Dove says. "Misha, like that Russian Blue. Or, he's made a mish-mash of things."

"The Mission." Dumpster announces. "Up on Dolores."

"Or Mission Street," Tallulah says.

I quiet them. "Maybe they are spotted. We need to consult with someone who has a bird's-eye view of the situation. Let us go."

"Where?" Dumpster asks, like I lead him to the end of the earth where cat food is not canned.

"Trust me."

In no time we complete our climb.

"Why you handsome old flatterer," says Miss Kitty when she sees me. "Did you come back to —" Then she sees the rest of the entourage.

"Not this time, Miss Kitty," I say, letting her down easy. "There is a new development in the kitnapping. I am hopeful that you can assist us monumentally."

She smooths her ruffled fur. "You can count on me, Sue Slate."

"Darlin' is missing and foul play is suspected."

"Fowl play?"

"No. *Foul* play."

"Ahhh," she says, with a mysterious air. "You must be talking about the bald-headed People in white who escorts somebody down the back steps. I cannot make out who it is, but it could be your Darlin'."

"Can this doc," I ask, "be the same gent all in white who is reported in the vicinity before?"

Dumpster says slowly, "I see a man all in white outside the Computer Moll's door one time."

"And you do not report this to me?"

"I'm off duty. It doesn't count."

"*You* have a small intestine for a brain, Demetrius Dumpster! Nevertheless, I entrust to you one small chore. You must alert Levis to the disappearance. Take this note. He may know if it is in Darlin's own hand."

"Oh, no!" cries Tallulah. "If not, then he may —"

"— have joined Big Ole!" Turtle Dove finishes. "Sue, does this doc do away with Big Ole too?"

"Calm down, everyone. We do not know that Darlin' is done away with. Or that Big Ole has a thing to do with it either. We must get to work and find out."

"Turtle Dove," instructs Dumpster, "you get Levis while I stand watch here."

"How can Turtle Dove get him to come?"

Dumpster polishes the backs of his claws against his pajamas. "I plan to send Esmeralda with her."

I nod. "This is a wise plan." Then I pause. "Wait one second, Dump. Turtle Dove is smaller than Esmeralda."

Dumpster shrugs. "It may take a while."

102

"Well, *we* cannot dally," I tell Tallulah. "To Mission *Street* without further ado!"

"Why?" asks Dumpster.

I fill him in briefly on the building with the white rooms. "Maybe this is where the phantom physician spirits our Darlin' boy to."

"Of course!" cries Tallulah. "I recall a room full of gleaming tubes and bottles! A laboratory!"

"Or a morgue if we do not hurry. Miss Kitty, my thanks to you. Come with me, powder puff."

Chapter 18

Normally I do not leave my alley more than once a month, for cultural events and the like. However, for the second time this P.M., or A.M., I am venturing down 14th Street, where it rains firepoppers. This time I propel a judy, and a precious one at that, so I do not go the mad dash routine. Almost losing Tallulah once is enough for yours truly.

At the corner of Clarion a figure lurches at us, but it is only a nip-soaked People who stumbles across the street. In a doorway two lovers rub and pet like alley cats. As we approach our target site we move single file from doorway to doorway, slower and slower.

I feel Tallulah's light touch on my tail.

"Stop, Sue."

The fur on my back is vertical with fear. I hope she does not notice.

"It smells familiar here."

I recall the sweet alyssum. "Good."

We enter the garden of weeds and steal through to a windowsill.

Whispering very softly Tallulah says, "This dark stench, like mossy stones. I was *here*, Sue." She grabs for my arm. "But so dizzy then!"

"Can you smell your way from here?" I see her hesitate. "Take your time. Sniff it out."

"Argh!" she cries, almost losing her balance.

A window screeched open.

"Can't you damn cats do your yowling somewhere else?"

Something smashes against the wall next to us.

"People!" I curse. "They can throw firepoppers till I go deaf, but a meow drives them nuts. Is it not obvious that we are saving the world?"

"Sue," Tallulah says, watching the window slam down. "Maybe we're not the first cats to disturb him. Maybe this is a heavy traffic area for meowing."

This is one smart chick. "I know that," I say.

Tallulah turns away as if to hide her face. Surely she does not laugh at me. She leads me inside the basement and up a short staircase.

"There is light up there," I note.

Strangely, there is also a cat door at the top of the stairs. I go through it first. I am astonished. On this floor there is carpeting up to my knees. The desk is no orange crate such as I possess, and without a doubt no one sits on shelves around here.

"Sue, this is it! I recognize the perfume!"

Then I notice the white shoes under the desk.

I almost leap to the ceiling when the voice speaks.

"Two more to check in, Doctor."

"Bring them in."

The voice sighs. "I wish you hadn't given those orderlies time off for the Fourth. *I* have to handle all these cats. *Vermin*," she mutters at us.

"All in a good cause."

I dare to look to the top of that white tower of People. She heads toward us. I look at my love. "Run, Tallulah!"

"No, Sue," she says. "I'm staying with you."

There is a crackling sound and the doctor's voice says, "Get their collars, throw them in the feeding room and then lock the subject entrance, Nurse Kling."

"Nurse Kling?" we ask each other. Surely this guardian of the evil place cannot be Rex Boudoir's *Mrs.* Kling?

She comes toward us in her jerky way, hands out like claws. That painted smile comes across her face, but still does not erase her sinister gleam. Her perfume — I cannot quite place it, but it reminds me of funerals. Indeed it *is* Rex's People, one and the same.

"Come pussies. Give me your collars and you'll get your feast."

"That voice," whispers Tallulah. "That voice —"

But I am pondering the collar business.

Rex's People comes closer, squinting at us over half-glasses. We back away, like a caterpillar in reverse. I signal to Tallulah.

Nurse Kling sees the light. "What is this? You *have* no collars. Who sent you here?"

We split up and make a run for it to either side of her. This tactic always succeeds with People. They have no smarts when it comes to dealing with feline brainpower. She lurches toward us and misses. We move again. And again. And again. By the time she figures it out, and tries just for me, we are under the desk.

"Try for the door when I do, Tallulah."

She answers with a sparkle in her eyes. This is some sweetpea, I think.

I hear the crackle again and know Nurse Kling is just seconds away from help if she thinks to call. We must penetrate the laboratory pronto. The inside door is as heavy as a semi filled with pallets of kitty litter. We fling ourselves against it, but it does not budge.

"Crabcakes!" I curse. My claws can find no place to grab.

"Doctor!" screeches Nurse Kling into the crackle box. "These are bogus cats!"

Bogus cats, indeed. If I am bogus how come the sound of the doctor's heavy footsteps convinces me I am about to die?

Nurse Kling keeps grabbing at us. We keep dodging. She trips over her chair and goes flying. Tallulah and I back up and wiggle our haunches.

"Now!" I yell and we fly through the legs at the door.

We are streaking down a long bright white corridor. There are doors everywhere. At the first open one we leap inside, the People hot on our tails.

Inside are cats. And cats. And more cats. Roary sleeps on a plush velour cushion under a heat lamp. Ethel nods across the room in a soaked-nip stupor. Others, bad news types from different neighborhoods, imbibe from a huge plate of nip. Everyone is either sacked out or eating.

And what a glorious spread. A trough of chicken livers cooked just this side of pink. Cheeses of every type lie here and there, half-devoured. Open cans of gourmet food. Whole fishies. An enormous bowl of raw shrimp.

But the People draw closer.

"Tallulah! Join the fun!"

Not ten seconds later Nurse Kling and the Doctor stand in the doorway. The doc is twice as broad as the nurse who is no slight person, and his blond fur almost touches the top of the doorway.

"Which ones?" he asks the nurse.

They are both checking out the room like it is an everyday affair to put on the dog for a platoon of cats.

"I don't know," claims the nurse. "They all look alike to me."

I risk a glance toward Tallulah Mimosa. She is sprawled across Yellow Ethel's lap staring glassy-eyed at the ceiling. Myself, I am stripping my fifth shrimp. Some of the joy is lost from this act, however, as I am aware that this may be my last meal ever.

"Think, woman! What did they look like?"

"Like every other piece of street vermin you drag in here. I don't know why you don't just cage them once you inject them with the FLV vaccine."

I choke on a shrimp.

"I need to have them in their accustomed environment, Nurse, to obtain a valid sample. Of course one can control disease in a lab. But most HIV patients aren't kept under glass, you know. If I'm ever going to find the link between the diseases, I have to lure the research animals back."

"Then get one of each and drown the duplicates. How else can I tell them apart? Though — no. One wore a green collar or something. I don't see it."

After one last look the doc shrugs. "Well, they're only cats. What harm can they do? We'll recruit them when they come out of hiding."

Only cats indeed, I think as we wait for them to vamoose.

The moment they disappear, Tallulah pulls her green scarf out from under a cushion. She sniffs her way down the hall.

"This is it!"

We scoot under a bed, staring at the doc's feet.

"I'm feeling great, Doc. When can I go home?" asks a barely audible voice.

"It's Darlin'!" I whisper to Tallulah.

"Now, now," says the doc. "You signed on for the whole experiment or nothing. I know we made that perfectly clear. Think of all the men you'll save by letting us follow up in a controlled setting." His voice leers. "Imagine how they'll show their gratitude to the brave men who tested the cure."

109

Another voice pipes up, "You've been saying that to us for months! If anything, staying on will make my health fail. I feel like a prisoner!"

"Now, now," answers the doc, nodding toward Nurse Kling.

"What about that man you took out of here earlier, Doc?" asks the patient. "Before you shot him up he was yelling that this was a prison, not a hospital; a graveyard, not a clinic. That we're human guinea pigs for some big drug company."

"You know what this disease can do to the brain. As a matter of fact, it sounds like *you're* showing some symptoms of cognitive impairment yourself. Let me give you something to keep you from worrying so much."

"No, Doc, no! I want to stay awake. I'm fine! Please, no more shots!" He backs away from the shining needle Nurse Kling wields.

"*This* will be your last, since you can't cooperate, buster. I've had enough trouble out of you."

"What do you mean?" Darlin' cringes.

"Inject him, Nurse, and we'll show this piece of human vermin what we mean."

Tallulah and I nearly collide as we leap out from under the bed. I slam on my brakes in front of the doc. He trips and nearly falls into Nurse Kling's outstretched arm.

"Damn cats! You could have killed me!" yells the doc.

The other patient is able to scramble away from the nurse. Tallulah leaps from the bed to the doc's bald spot. He spins around, trying to push Tallulah off his head, and trips over me again. He falls face forward.

Nurse Kling stares at him. He does not move.

Chapter 19

Nurse Kling screams bloody murder in the doorway. Darlin' still stares.

"What's in that hype to make him so frightened?" Darlin' asks. "Would it really kill you?"

The patient shakes his head. "Not right off. It seems somehow to reverse the progress of the drugs they've given us."

"Drugs which work?"

"Better than anything else so far."

Running down the corridor, Nurse Kling screams, "Help police! Help po —!" She stops in mid-word. In all likelihood she realizes the value of not alerting the law to this sinister operation.

Now Darlin' gives us the once-over. "Did you kitties *know*?"

I am washing the shrimp juice off my face; Tallulah is likewise occupied.

There is commotion at the end of the hallway.

"You can't come in here!" Nurse Kling shouts.

Darlin' shrinks into the wall like a shadow.

In a moment, panting in the doorway, is the cavalry. Levis, wearing a long black cape, and in his arms Esmeralda.

"Darlin'!" he cries.

"Thank goodness you found me!"

"I thought you might want your bear."

I wink at Tallulah. "Dumpster and Turtle Dove to the rescue!" I whisper.

In Levis's arms, Darlin' babbles. "I was so wrong! I believed the doctor. I thought he had a cure, but now I see he was using us. This man says they're luring gay men here for experimentation, literally sacrificing us to develop a cure for breeders. I believe it. This place is an armed camp and the orderlies are guards! Oh, this couldn't happen if the FDA were sane!"

"Who is this?" asks Levis, pointing to the doc.

Darlin' explains quickly. He gloms us. "I'd swear these two attacked him and saved my life. What did you do, raise a fur-covered army?"

Levis laughs, then talks a blue streak. "No, but these alley cats around my building are something else. Sometimes I think all we people have to do is sit back and let them run the world." He bends to pick me up. "Madonna has been a lifesaver. She

113

always knows when I'm at my worst because there she'll be, curled up beside me."

"She does the same for me," says Darlin', his soft voice like a lullaby. I guess that he appreciates me. "Sting too. It's a wonder he's not here."

"*He* was sitting on your teddy bear. In my apartment."

"How did it get there?"

"I thought maybe you dropped it off."

"No. I left her behind." He thinks for a minute. "But how did you know where to come?"

"You mentioned Ricky and Tom. I called Ricky's lover who was no easy nut to crack. He'd been sworn to secrecy but he slipped with the cross street when I told him I knew from your message that it was on Mission. Esmeralda and I looked for a place with lights on this time of night. And got invited to a swinging party in one building."

"I'm so glad you didn't go," sighs Darlin', his mitt in Levis's, stars in his eyes.

Down the hall Mrs. Kling screams into the phone. I suspect reinforcements are on her agenda. I rub Levis's ankles. He looks down.

"You know," he says, "I think we ought to take advantage of this lull and absent ourselves from the scene of the crime."

Tallulah is at the door, fluffy as I ever see her, staring at the boys.

"I do not believe your cats. You want us out of here right *now*, don't you, kitties?"

Darlin' tries to rise from the bed. "Whew. I think the knock-out medications they've been giving me have done just that. My legs feel like Gumby rejects."

I jump into a wheelchair.

114

Levis notices and shoos me out of it. "Cab, sir?" he asks Darlin'.

"No, I'll just hold you up. There may be others here who need to be sprung."

"And we haven't got a thing to tell the cops except this place is probably unlicensed and you and I are standing over what looks like a dead body."

Speaking of the dead, the doc groans and starts to stir.

I check the hall. Nothing is doing. Levis wheels Darlin' out, but Tallulah's not with them. I stay put. Levis looks at me. He turns to look into the room. Tallulah is at her post, clawing at the keys on the doc's belt while he groans and waves her away. Levis zips in to unhook them, pats Tallulah and says, "All right, kitties. Can we go now?"

We pass the orgy room. Empty. Trouble always knows trouble.

Speaking of trouble, sauntering out of another room, Bad Tuna Gat, big as life and twice as mean, settles like a thunderhead in front of us, the fur boiling from his ears like steam. I know I am in for it as there is no way this cat ever forgets that I see him at his weakest, sobbing for Big Ole.

"What are you doing here, you striated emasculated excuse for a woman?" he growls. He still has a hint of his kitty lit vocabulary from the days before he learns that crime is more lucrative.

"I am leading my People to freedom."

"You muff-divers really stick with your kind, don't you?"

"I see your paid lackeys abscond on you when the going gets tough."

"I dismiss them, top-sergeant," he sniggers. "Take

115

care of anybody's privates lately?" he asks, looking at Tallulah.

It is all I can do not to smash his potato face in, talking like this in front of Tallulah. But he is Persian and his face is thereby already punched-in. "What do you want, Bad Tuna?"

"I want the cash the Doc stashes."

"What cash?"

"*What* cash," he mimics me. "The bread he utilizes to operate this gay drug bar. Don't play dumb on me, *marimacho*. What else are you doing here?"

"What about you? You are everywhere these days. At the Church, here, even at," I decide to risk it to see what response I get, "Big Ole's. It seems like you cannot be in all these places without some business at each. And I do not believe it stops at dirty money. Which is not in my possession."

"Dogshit. You got it stashed in your boxer shorts? Take 'em off, Slate. Show the lady what's missing. Or does she already know?"

"That is enough, Gat," I say. In the flick of a whisker I turn and slug him with both back feet at once. He careens from wall to wall in the hallway all the time we make our escape.

Chapter 20

It is no coincidence that the reception area is empty. Yellow Ethel is in another room hanging by her claws from Nurse Kling's head. Leonora may not approve, but it looks like her prodigy finally realizes her feline potential.

Ethel motions for us to skedaddle. I bless the little catnip-head.

As easy as locating turkey in a pot pie, we find the front exit and plow down the steps.

Chilly fog leans over Mission Street. I have the shivers.

"Maybe we can find a cab," says Darlin'.

Levis laughs. "On Mission Street at two A.M.? With two feline passengers? Are you kidding — Darlin'? *Darlin'!*"

I flash on the commotion. Darlin' is having a convulsion that is second fiddle to any I witness before. He turns deadweight in the chair. Levis holds him. "Come back, Prince Charmin', we have to get out of here."

Indeed, I am becoming antsy hanging around outside this den of vipers. Darlin' starts to come around, groggy and mumbling.

Tallulah paces back and forth at Darlin's feet. I race ahead. Stop. Race ahead again until Levis notices.

He stares at me like I just discover gravity. "Is this really happening?" he asks, his voice like a speeded up record. "You want me to follow again, Madonna? Maybe that was the wrong name for you. You look more like Daisy Diesel-Dyke." I am so pleased I almost forget to be nervous. "Next thing I know Tinkerbell will light my way and Wonderwoman will punish the villains." He pushes Darlin' along. "Come to think of it, make it Batman instead and I'll take this whole fantasy."

Mission Street feels like an empty bag at this hour of the A.M. No more firepoppers. However, it is like being the bull's-eye on a target. Levis is not used to the chair. He is slow as disintegrating birdie offal. At the first corner he almost dumps Darlin' out on the curb.

Then we hear it. The screech of brakes.

"Dalmation!" curses Tallulah.

Levis zips Darlin' into a doorway.

I look at Tallulah. She apologizes for her French.

As we cower Nurse Kling exits the laboratory like a cat on a hot tin roof.

"About time you numbskulls got here!" She holds a towel to her head upon which Ethel leaves her John Hancat.

"Ah, dry up, Florence Nightingale. I don't know why the Company let you Bible freaks in on this." The man looks like a sack of kibble with legs. He checks out the street. "They *have* to be inside. Where can a couple of dying perverts go this time of night?"

"Dying perverts," mutters Levis.

A towering beanpole rushes up the steps after Burly and the nurse. He hits his head on the top of the doorway, staggers back, bends and runs inside.

I am out of the doorway in a flash, zipping across the street and up Mission, cursing the bright neon signs which light us up like spotlights. Tallulah is by my side, Levis right behind us, pushing Darlin' as fast as he can.

At Sixteenth I aim uphill. Tallulah drops back to watch for pursuers. Levis steamrolls along, full wheelchair ahead. I stop on Caledonia Street to wait. Darlin' slumps lower than a summer moon. Levis tries to prop him up without stopping and plows into three garbage cans. I never hear a crash so loud. He dumps Darlin' and Esmeralda onto the sidewalk.

"Jesus H —" shouts Levis.

The smackup brings Darlin' fully around.

Tallulah sprints to us. "The car stops when they hear the crash! They are headed this way!"

Sparrow Street is a tiny strip just around the

corner. Levis tips the cans up, drops one. The car sounds closer than a major quake. There is no time to upend the can. Levis wheels the chair onto Sparrow, then throws himself across Darlin's lap.

Chapter 21

When Burly and the Beanpole drive by we are all three in doorways and flat as fishcakes. The night is darker than a mile down a Doberman's throat. Tallulah elects to stay exposed. She is out by the upturned can, chewing on something nasty.

Then I see it: Esmeralda lies on the curb. I pray Nurse Kling does not pick up on this detail. Why does Darlin' have to choose a screaming green bear?

When Burly shines his light on Tallulah she raises her fur and hisses. Nurse Kling squints from the car, but even yours truly cannot peg Tallulah Mimosa. My admiration for her abounds.

"It's only alley riffraff, you jerks!" Nurse Kling complains. "The cat knocks over a can and you think your search is over. Get a move on!" She is bopping the driver on the head with a rolled up magazine. She is so mad she does not direct her searchlight to our doorways or at the telltale teddy bear. The old bucket lurches forward.

We hold the frieze longer than it takes cheese to mold. Tallulah whispers about the foul taste in her mouth.

"I don't have to eat garbage any more, thanks to Big Mom. I'm not used to it."

I am about to go stir bugs when the boys start whispering.

"Ricky and Tom wouldn't tell me where the lab they were checking into was or who ran it," explains Darlin'. "See, the FDA was not interested in seriously pursuing cures, but these people were, they said. Then, when I started having trouble getting around, I got a visit from Big Ole. Well, the man's no great loss to the gay world, let me tell you, but he's very nice, and company, so he visited me a few times. I made it *very* clear that I did not intend to recant my sexuality. Then he came in all excited one day. He pitched this new lab. I was so pleased to get a lead on it I asked him to check up on my friends. He claimed they were doing extremely well. But he wouldn't let me visit them because of security."

"Security — ha!" Levis smirks.

"One day," Darlin' continues, "Ole came over looking very shaky. He said nothing was wrong, but he also didn't talk about the lab, which had been our main topic for days. He just kept looking more and more worried and left soon. The very next day I heard he'd been murdered."

The night feels like a wet blanket closing in on us. Everything is muted but Burly and the Beanpole's tires, which sound like cornered mice squealing around corners, farther and farther away from the rescue crew.

Darlin' asks, "What do you think was going on? Who's behind this?"

"They talk about a Company. And then there's Big Ole and Nurse Kling. And we gay guinea pigs."

"Dispensable," Darlin' repeats, shaking his pate. "They want a cure for the human race, but we're subhuman. They've found a way to use the virus as a lethal cure for their hate."

"We've always been dispensable," Levis agrees.

Darlin' steps out of his chair and stands tall. "No more," he says in an angry growl. "I may not live another six months, but while I'm here, I'll count."

I shepherd my flock out of Sparrow Street.

Chapter 22

At 5:30 in the morning, our entourage finally arrives at Peacock Alley. Tallulah and Numero Uno take a back seat to the proceedings as we already attract more attention than is wise, albeit for an excellent cause. We huddle on the fire escape to watch.

The Computer Moll and Ethan, with his French poodle, pine on Levis's sectional couch and look like they are going through the wars. When the key hits the lock the Moll leaps up, earrings jingling and flashing, and pulls the door open.

"You're back!" she hollers so loud she drowns out the garbage truck which is clanging to a halt below us. Dawn creeps into San Francisco.

Darlin' staggers in, Levis on his tail. Ethan flings the poodle and hugs them both. Then he steps back and glares at Darlin'.

"If I find that you have simply been out *tricking* all night —"

But he pipes down. Darlin' looks about as white as Miss Kitty. Ethan turns to the couch and starts to plump pillows and offer sustenance.

At the sound of pawsteps on the stairs behind us I spin, ready to take care of Bad Tuna once and for all. It is only Dumpster and Turtle Dove.

"Did you see? Did you see?" the Dump asks with more excitement in his voice than I hear in a millennium. "My scheme works!" He points to green Esmeralda in Darlin's arms.

"What do you mean, *your* scheme?" squeaks Turtle Dove. Her gold lamé sees better nights than this, having tufts of feathers and spots of fire escape rust as decoration. "You know perfectly well it is I who sees the bear first. I adore that green."

"Can't you find a riddle to tell?" barks Dumpster. He is chewing on a stogie.

Turtle Dove pouts, then tosses her chin in the air, whiskers a-tremble. "As a matter of fact —" and before I can silence her, she is off and running. I take a gander inside the windows, but the People are absorbed.

"A little piece of string goes into a bar," says Turtle Dove, "and orders a drink. The bartender says, 'We don't serve no strings here.' The little string is crushed. She goes outside and ponders what to do.

125

Then another string comes by. 'What is wrong?' asks the other string. The little string weeps out her sad story. 'Aw, you just do not know how,' says the new string. She ruffles her top, ruffles her bottom, ties herself up and rolls into the bar. She orders a beer. The bartender gives her the beer, looks again and says, 'Wait a minute, aren't you a string?' The string answers, 'I'm afraid not!' " Turtle Dove stifles her laughter.

Tallulah sighs, "Coddess help us."

The People finish rehashing their night.

Ethan asks, "I don't understand what Mrs. Kling has to do with all this. I thought she was really nice, and loved kitties."

Tallulah rolls her eyes.

The Computer Moll runs her hand over her crewcut. "She's been visiting me too and I'm not even sick. And she is always dragging that conceited cat of hers along. The red one she insists is a show cat. If manners win ribbons, he's never won a thing."

Ah-ha! Then perhaps Rex loses his jewels after visiting the Moll, who lives right under Big Ole, and has nothing to do with the murder.

The Moll keeps talking. "I wished she wouldn't bring that cat along. He wouldn't stay on her lap and insisted on exploring every inch of the apartment."

"Was he after the parrot?" asks Levis.

"Never gave her a glance," she answers with her little dry cough. "He usually settled for sprawling over Alice's keyboard, or cozying up to her air vents if I'd left her on."

"You don't think," Levis begins. "No. That's impossible."

"What?" asks Ethan. "Something is going on that

126

we don't understand. I think we need to look at the unlikely things since the likely isn't making a bit of sense."

I am hot to get in there and kick Levis into talking. If he has ideas about Rex, he is on the right track.

Levis rubs his stubble. "But how could Mrs. Kling even know about our network?"

"What network?" asks Ethan.

Out on the fire escape, the four of us ask one another, "What network?"

Chapter 23

"Does this have something to do with the way you two disappear all the time? Have you been up there computer-worshipping?" Darlin' asks.

The Moll and Levis look at each other.

"We might as well tell them," says the Moll, sighing like this is tortured out of her.

Levis slips his cape off and folds his dukes on his knees. "It all began when it became obvious that the Feds were not going to allocate precious funds — that could, after all, be used to wage war — for something as positive as AIDS research."

The Moll takes it up. "And put that together with how the pharmaceutical firms believe in profits, not people —"

"We formed a group called the Variant Entries."

"What a scream!" whispers Turtle Dove.

"Which is the AIDS research arm of an international gay computer club. We wanted to at least see what we could do in the way of advancing research from the molasses stage to something that moved a little faster by eliminating red tape and adding that extra oomph of extreme motivation."

"It just made sense to us," says the Moll, "that if some of the smartest people in the world are gay, and if they were particularly invested in finding a cure, it had to work."

"The scientists had already been gathering data, but each one was stuck in his or her specialty, like vaccines vs. cures, the virus itself or the related infections, the immune system or even the spiritual aspects of the disease."

"You mean they didn't already have access to information through computers?" asks Darlin', his voice even more soft than usual.

"Sure they did, but you know how protective the drug companies are of anything that'll make money, or governments are unless they're getting an equal trade. It was just after my breakup," says the Moll, tears popping into her dark eyes. "I was able to donate my skills and time with no holds barred and found out a lot of others were also. With our network we could connect the gay researchers from every firm, every country, especially France, who were willing to subvert their official allegiances, their funding sources, to work with other gay researchers."

She hangs her head. "But I have to confess something about Mrs. Kling. I thought she was harmless."

"Uh-oh," says Darlin'.

"I do not want to hear this," says Turtle Dove.

The Moll goes on, with her little cough. "I didn't exactly describe what we're doing. This was several months ago, in the very beginning. I was very excited and was waiting for an important transmission and here was this perfectly innocent-seeming — but how did she even know to visit me in the first place? She didn't show up until after the project started."

Levis said, "Who knows? A spy? Someone working in a lab with our people? It doesn't matter. Once she knew this was the place where the data was coordinated all she had to do was gain access. And goodness knows that's easy enough to do; it doesn't take much cash these days to buy the codes that'll break into a system, whether from an insider or an ace computer raider who can figure them out."

"I'm afraid you're right."

Tallulah is leaning against me. "I do not know," I tell her, "where this is leading, but I am not encouraged, to say the very least."

Darlin's voice is like a cat's tongue on sandpaper. "This is incredible. Never mind the spies. So you dudes are working on a cure too? Madame Curie and Madame Curie?"

"You bet. For insurance as much as anything. When the big boys come up with something, we want at least to know enough to force its testing and make sure it's accessible to everyone. If a vaccine or whatever can be duplicated, then no one can control

130

it for profit, withhold it by bureaucratic bumbling or use it to kill off queers."

Tallulah asks, "What is a queer?"

Dumpster spits out stogie rawhide. "People have the brain power of Scottie dogs. They think love is queer."

I elucidate. "They think they know better than the Coddess and decide it is wrong to have a paramour of the same sexual gender."

"Like us?" asks Tallulah, looking into my eyes.

"Queer as six-toed cats!" says Turtle Dove.

Levis grabs a fistful of computer disks from his desk. "These," he says, "may save us all!"

"Oh-h . . ." I say.

"What?" whispers Tallulah.

"This is what I find on day one, in Big Ole's water heater. I am certain at the time that my discovery breaks the case."

"Our hero!" I hear. But then I realize it is not Tallulah who croons this out, but Dumpster, in a ridiculous falsetto.

I kick paint chips at him on my way in the window. The disk is just where I leave it, under the rug. I work it free. The tap-dancing cats clatter upstairs while I save the world.

I dangle the disk in front of Levis.

"Hey, Rosie the Riveter! Good girl." He turns to the Computer Moll. "Did you give Madonna a disk to play with?"

The Moll comes at me, jingling, like I am not begging to give the thing to her.

"Where did you find this, kitty?" she asks, getting to her knees. I drop it and retreat. "It's like ours,

131

gang. I need to check it out on the screen, though. And in the shape it's in, I'm not sure what we can see."

"Do you mean someone might have swiped one?" asks Ethan.

"At least one," says Levis. "What are we waiting for?"

Darlin' hefts himself up. Ethan helps. "Are you well enough to travel, doll?"

"Up a flight of stairs? What do you take me for, a sissy?"

"Well," says Ethan, dangling the poodle under his arm, "as a matter of fact —"

"Sic him, Justine," Darlin' says with a toss of his head.

I rejoin the conspiracy on the fire escape. Dumpster thumps me on the back with his tail. "Coup furry," he says in his fake French. But I am pondering. Why does the God Is Not Dead Church hire Ethan? They are the ones who pass out tracts against People like him, yet they tolerate this one.

Then I notice Levis, looking straight at us out the fire escape.

"Whoops," says Turtle Dove. She backs to the stairs.

Levis is gesturing for us to follow, though, and holding the door open to the hall.

"It would appear that the jig is up," I tell them. "Let us join the party."

The four mouserteers mount the windowsill, jump into the apartment and file through the door.

Levis whispers to me, "Who are you, Supercat?"

I fervently hope that Tallulah hears.

Chapter 24

"What in the world did you bring all those cats for?" Ethan asks when we are assembled at the Computer Moll's computer.

"Ah," says Levis like he is announcing the Saturday night mystery show on KPAU Radio. "The cats are the key."

"You silly boy," says Ethan. Does he look worried?

The Computer Moll looks like a sorcerer stirring a disgusting brew. But she does not stir, she pokes, at Alice-the-computer's keys.

Ethan still gives with strange stares. "The way your fur people are watching the screen, you'd think you were waiting for a Tom and Jerry cartoon."

"*Mission Impossible* is more like it," mumbles Darlin' with a wink at me.

"*I* prefer *I Love Lucy* reruns," announces Turtle Dove. Dumpster swats at her.

"*Don't* muss my whiskers, you brute! I just curled them!"

The Computer Moll scopes out the screen. With a cough she says, "This *is* our disk." I note no little anger smoldering in her voice.

Tallulah looks at me with eyes as wide as the moon in heat.

"It is, guys," the Computer Moll confirms. "Remember that disk that just disappeared? Levis, you and Ethan had a terrible fight that night because you were so upset about its loss. And the darned cat had it. Why don't you try birds?"

"I'm not so sure the cat, at least this cat, took it," says Levis. "Anyway, thank goodness it's back. Paris will be relieved."

"Paris?" asks Darlin'.

"That's the lab that made this breakthrough. And it was a big one."

"I'll go ahead and put it through now. If no one relieved us of the data already on here."

"Shouldn't we find out who stole it?" asks Ethan. "Or how it got here?"

The People go into a huddle.

"Sue?" whispers Tallulah.

As per usual this doll's voice raises the fur at the base of my tail.

134

"Maybe someone steals the disks to use the cures themselves and doesn't let them reach our side?"

I ponder this.

Dumpster, who not two shakes of a dog's tail ago I hear wheezing in his sleep, leaps up, races to the wastebasket and tumbles it down. Then he grabs a big piece of paper and wrestles it behind the couch where one and all can hear him shredding, shredding, shredding.

"What's with that one?" asks Ethan.

Dumpster leaves his tail in sight and thumps it as he shreds.

"Good work," I tell him.

"Rain de toot."

The poodle whips his curly little gray head around.

"Parley voo?" he squawks.

"Now the dog has to start," the Moll complains.

"Key parley voo?" asks the poodle.

Levis is giving a long look-see at Dumpster's tail. Then he shouts, "By Jove, I think he's got it! They're shredding our data!"

"What are you talking about, honey?" Ethan asks. "I think you are *all* nutty as fruitcakes. And I know I'm not far off the mark. Cats, computers, secret clinics — this is madness!"

Ethan's little beaver-face looks so innocent.

"Don't you see," insists Levis. "Mrs. Kling comes up here regularly enough to get an idea of when the important transmissions are expected."

The Computer Moll groans and beats her head against the screen.

"She lets the gang know, they somehow lift the right disk and steal the information."

"How would they know the right disk?" asks Darlin'.

The Moll answers. "Probably from Mrs. Kling's spy work. She'd always take forever separating her cat from Alice. That gave her time to observe what was current."

Darlin' says, "So that's how the clinic pulled its wonders on the boys they worked with before eliminating them." His voice slows for the first time in three years. "But how, if the clinic had the same stuff as you, did they get so far ahead?"

Levis goes to Dumpster and picks up the shredded paper. "This is how. They'd copy the disk for themselves, then alter it and send it out on the modem."

The room goes as silent as a pilgrim to Puss'n'Boots' memorial.

"No!" cries the Computer Moll. "Do you realize what this means? We've thought we were gaining on the damned virus again and again when the rug's been pulled out from under our feet. No wonder we aren't getting anywhere. The receivers are getting worthless data."

"But," asks Darlin', "how does Kling and her bunch tap in?"

"All they needed was one disk to get the field," she explains.

"Quawk!"

It is my turn to groan. Dolly Parrot is covered by night. Consequently I presume myself to be safe. But now the sun claws her way up the sky and leaves big tears in the fog. The birdbrain stirs at the light.

"*Catbandit!*" she shrieks beneath her cover.

The Computer Moll pulls off her sheet. "She's just upset at all the furry visitors."

"But didn't you say that Rex is always up here?"

"There's only one of him."

"*Catbandit!*"

I never catch this phrase in Dolly's vocabulary prior to today. The bird cocks her head this way and that, flapping her gross black tongue around in her beak, performing her morning elimination rituals for all assembled.

"*Not* on the floor again, Dolly," complains the Computer Moll. "She does this when she wants attention."

"*Catbandit! Catbandit! Catbandit!*"

Levis steps to the cage. "Pardon me, Dolly, but has a cat been sneaking around here?"

Dolly flaps her wings and gawks at the room. She rolls her eyes like a slot machine which flips out. "*Catbandit!*"

Levis turns to me. I zero in on a spot between my toes with my tongue. Levis takes a seat cross-legged in front of me.

I lick for a long time indeed, struggling with my dilemma. Can I trust this People? What is the consequence to our lives? I think of my beloved Tallulah, of eccentric Turtle Dove, of good old reliable Dumpster, even of pitiful, hate-filled Bad Tuna Gat. People flash on feline powers in ancient Egypt and such-like advanced civilizations, but if something does not fit into human understanding it is ignored — or destroyed. Which is it for us if I spill the beans?

Levis is special. Not only is he my People, but he is as fey as a drag queen at Mardi Gras. He bends to

137

me and whispers, "I'll cover for you. Just start walking."

I take my time with the rest of my bath. It is imperative that the crowd does not assume my actions to be related to Levis's. Then I rise and make my way to the door, which I rub like the sandbox is an urgent destination.

In a loud whisper Levis tells the others, "Let's follow Madonna. Maybe she'll *inadvertently* lead us to some information. After all, she's the one who found the disk."

I march ahead, musing. What I consider while making my decision is that this can save many lives. The People are forgetting that their data is mixed at the clinic with more from the drug company: our cure. This is the risk I weigh mightily and take.

Chapter 25

I lead the People out the porch door. They file behind me silent as mice stealing catfood crumbs. It is one of those San Francisco days when the wind is up. The eucalyptus branches flail. Levis throws the cape over his shoulders and it flies out behind him. Kites already appear in the sky. Clouds race over us. One minute we are in shadow and it is almost night again, the next minute sunlight pours down like gold.

I ascend to Big Ole's. At the top of the stairway is his water heater. I make for it, stretch up, sink my claws into the insulation. I tear off a hunk of the stuff. The People huddle, watching me, looking at one another like they all question their sanity, unaware that this is the most sane action of their various and sundry lives. Like a one-bird band, Morty Mockingbird serenades Peacock Alley.

I toss my insulation in the air, catch it, roll over, catch it in my claws.

"That's how you played with the disk," says Levis.

Then I carry the insulation in my teeth to the water heater. I do my best to stuff it back in.

"Well, well," says Ethan, "the cat wouldn't come back to Ole's to tear that thing apart if it didn't get positive reinforcement before. It must have found something to play with."

The Computer Moll asks, "Could the disk have been hidden here?"

I repeat my pantomime over and over.

"It certainly looks like that," Darlin' determines.

"Which means," says Levis, "that Ole may have had something to do with this."

"Yes," adds Ethan in a breathless voice. "Enough so that he was murdered!" He steps back, holding tightly to Justine. Everyone turns to him except Levis, who continues to watch me.

"So if Ole was hyping the clinic to you, Darlin'," Levis says, "he was connected to them. And the clinic was working with AIDS cures. And we were working with AIDS cures. And the cat found one of your disks on Ole's back porch. Hidden, I guess we can assume."

I wish to pat the man on his little head, but as this is impossible, I rub against his ankles.

The tension in the group lessens. The Computer Moll asks, "If they already took the information off,

140

why didn't they just return the altered disk like they must have all the others?"

Levis looks at me. I have no answer for him, but just then Turtle Dove sashays over and begins to lick Dumpster. I am embarrassed to death in front of Tallulah.

"That gold cat," Levis asks, "is it male? I know Sting is."

Ethan bends down to check. "They're both boys! Talk about exhibitionism!"

"Didn't you tell me," Levis asks Ethan, "that you were once lovers with Ole?"

Ethan nods. "Yes, eons ago. How I adored that man. He'd give you the shirt off your back if you needed it and he was so good to me. That Church was the ruin of him and I introduced him to it, dragging him along on my watering runs. I thought it'd be fun to screw around in the fundamentalists' own lair. Now he's been mixed up in all this. He certainly didn't deserve the end he got."

"What if he thought he was doing some good?" Levis says. Turtle Dove, now that her point is made, starts on her own under-the-tail. "What if he really cared about people with AIDS? And then discovered that part of the operation involved knocking off gay guinea pigs? How would he react?"

"He'd get out as fast as he could," Ethan replies. "And pull their covers."

"A good reason for murder," the Computer Moll says quietly.

I rub against Levis again. Tallulah helps with the other leg. If we can just get the People to Mrs. Kling's I am willing to give odds that they deduce more.

141

"This is no time to beg for breakfast, kitty," says Darlin'.

Dumpster's eyes open like hungry jaws. Darlin' says the magic word: breakfast. The Dump begins to rub too, albeit for his own purposes.

Ethan looks at Dumpster with a wink. "I always get hungry afterwards too," he says, looking toward Turtle Dove who is licking her lips.

Now that three of us urge the People in one direction, they seem to catch on. We lead them downstairs, then up more stairs. All around us pigeons rise from their roosts like divine escorts.

At Rex's pad I check out a window. Mrs. Kling is slumped over the breakfast table looking like her night does not go well. Rex sits on a window above us, preening himself in a dusty sun ray. There is a scent of Gourmet Feast in the air. I kick Dumpster to keep him from an untimely assault on the kitchen. Rex's collar flashes in the sun. All sorts of tacks and clips hang off it. It is a wonder Rex still has the power to open his neat little cat door.

I get into my toreador act and charge said door, wishing I have a red cape to swirl. I charge again and again until Rex notices. He is a sucker for showing off and jumps down to exit his door, then reenter, easy as pie.

The Computer Moll gets it. "It's one of those pet doors that's activated by a magnet. That obnoxious cat was always draping himself over Alice. I was afraid the magnet would erase everything in her."

Levis says, "Maybe that was the point. I think we've come to the right place." He knocks on the door.

Mrs. Kling moves slowly. As she opens the door

the sun disappears again. She is out of uniform. Her bathrobe looks like silk.

"Why, what a surprise!" she croons. "Visitors. To what do I owe this honor?" Then she realizes where she sees Levis and Darlin' before. She looks down at us and I think she is going to shut the old slammer in all our little vermin faces.

We move in, like Glenn Gull's friends circling in a storm. Just then the front doorbell rings. Mrs. Kling raises her hands to her head as if in panic, looking from us to the front door and back again. The front door opens.

"Big Mom!" cries Tallulah.

Mrs. Kling does not act half so happy. "I've told you never to darken my doorstep again, Karen!"

Big Mom is sobbing her heart out. Tallulah Mimosa runs to her.

"Patches!" cries Big Mom. She picks Tallulah up and cuddles her. "Patches. All I have left in the world!"

Then she examines Tallulah. "What are you doing with this green scarf around your neck? Isn't it part of one I gave to this sister of mine?"

"Sister?" says Dumpster.

"Sister?" says Darlin'.

"Sister?" whispers the Computer Moll.

In a twinkling I, Sue Slate, Private Eye, see what I should notice previous to this moment, a resemblance between the two People. Before I note only differences. Icy Mrs. Kling and her show cat being sugary sweet to everyone from their pricey top floor apartment. Big Mom in her droopy thrift-shop cardigans in the basement, taking in all the stray alley cats. But their faces are as alike as two kittens

143

from the same litter. And at last I know where Big Ole gets his "Obsession."

Big Mom seems to see the rest of us for the first time. "I guess you already have company. We'll talk later. But don't think I'm going to let this pass. If you don't go to the police," she whispers in a threatening tone, "I *will!* I don't care if you're family!"

Chapter 26

Ethan moves to Big Mom then and puts an arm around her. "You may want to stay, Mom. It's about Ole."

"If it's to watch some kind of come-uppance for this cold-hearted bitch I'll gladly stay."

"Get out, Karen!"

Ethan ushers Big Mom in. She sits on the couch, Tallulah on her lap. I move in next to Tallulah like she is an electric heater.

Turtle Dove joins us, digging a crater into the

slipcover before she relaxes. Mrs. Kling looks ready to execute her too.

"Psst, Sue," says Turtle Dove. "Do you hear about the tom who goes before the judge for assault?"

"This is not the time, Dove."

"Levity *never* hurts. The judge asks his name, occupation and charge. The prisoner says *I'm Sparky, I work as an electrician and the charge is battery, please show me mercy!* The judge answers, *Put him in a dry cell!*"

She has the smarts to giggle quietly.

Levis asks Big Mom, "Why were you planning to call the police?"

"These people have *got* to be stopped, that's why," answers Big Mom. Hanging off her head is a thick braid of hair she is wringing like a wet rope. With her other hand she gives Tallulah the deep massage I am interested in administering. "It's not just my poor son, may he rest in peace finally now that *your* employers have killed him, dear sister of mine. It's all the gay people who must be saved from your hatred. Every one of them has a mother who will mourn like me."

"Very pretty speech, Karen, but you'd better shut up. I'm warning you," says Mrs. Kling, stepping menacingly toward us.

But Big Mom won't dummy up. She says to Darlin', "You poor, poor boys. First you get so sick, then they want to experiment on you like Nazis. And they killed my boy Ole because he tried to tell them how wrong they are."

"Ole?" asks Levis. "Ole was your son?"

"Ole?" says Turtle Dove.

"Didn't you all know?" says Ethan.

"I thought everyone knew that. Oh, I know at the last he acted more like *her* then me, but inside he was like me, just a plain soul. I had to give him to *her* to raise when I went to prison for five years. Yes, this sweet old lady has paid her dues behind bars. But the robberies Big Mom's mob pulled off were nothing compared to the mistake I made leaving an impressionable human being with *her*. *She* planted the seeds for him to turn into one of those close-minded born-agains by filling him with guilt and confusion. *She* did terrible things to keep him from the boy he loved. Why, anyone can love, I learned that in prison. I loved a lady there more than I could ever love a man and when she's released she's coming right here to be with me. I wish she could've known Ole, known him as he was before *she* lured him with that survivalist nonsense about the pure being saved after the day of judgment."

Mrs. Kling's face is redder than the sun in smog. She throws razors at her sister with her eyes.

"She's been obsessed by gays for years," Big Mom goes on regardless. "Ever since her husband left her for a beautiful man twenty years her junior, it's been her personal mission to chase every last one of us out of San Francisco. She and that misguided band at her church. They think the nuclear holocaust will purge their world — of course she wouldn't stop at killing someone!"

Just then Dumpster, who is MIA for quite some time at my request, comes to the window. He dumps the rhinestones I found on Big Ole's staircase in front of me. I play with them, tossing them, making sure one lands at Mrs. Kling's feet.

She bolts up. She stares at them like they are poison snakes about to strike. Now I know for sure that Rex loses them. Kling is probably in a tizzy all along, afraid Rex loses them in just the wrong spot. Her panic causes this Jesus-moll to flip.

"It was an accident, I tell you!" she shouts. "I called the police and reported finding him. His dear old aunt just paying a visit to get the 'Obsession' Ole bought me. You wouldn't want the cops to know it was *his* perfume, would you? And telling them it was for me explained my fingerprints, everything. They never guessed I did anything more than find him! That I had to knock him out so I could brain him with a brick I found on his back porch. I wrapped it in a towel first, and washed the towel."

"Pretty clever," says Dumpster. "No evidence. I have to remember that trick."

Mrs. Kling backs toward her bathroom door. At first I think she intends to take it on the lam, but she ducks inside the sandbox and comes out in thirty seconds with a hypo in her mitt.

"Not again," Levis sighs.

Now she maneuvers toward the back door. We all tense. "Stay back, toots, this can get nasty," I warn Tallulah.

"I am a big girl, Sue."

"Yeah, that's why I love you. But indulge me on this one."

"Why don't you give me that?" Levis says to Mrs. Kling.

"Why? So you can lock me up too, like this ne'er-do-well sister of mine?" She jabs toward him with the hypo. "For what? For ridding San Francisco of you vermin? The church thought we would run

148

you out with the law, but then you took over the government. We tried to purge the government and got nothing but a martyr. The Lord wanted us to take His work into our own hands. Ole was our instrument. A reformed pansy who could persuade you to do what we wanted: turn your filthy selves over to Future Pharmaceuticals. They make veterinary medicine. They suspected a tie between Feline Leukemia Virus and AIDS, but they needed human subjects as well as feline subjects. For this they knew they'd have to have neighborhood allies who could identify you queers."

She was jabbing the hypo toward Ethan as she talked, moving closer and closer to him.

"You used me!" he said. "I thought I was bridging communities and you were just making lists of the names and bars I'd mention!"

"Just as I deduce," I tell Tallulah. "Ethan is not tolerated at the God Is Not Dead. He is just innocent and chatty."

"That was just the beginning! We had a publicity campaign to discredit all other cures so you would depend only on Future. We were going to get anything off the market or out of commission that eased the misery of the disease, physical or spiritual, so more and more patients would go for the Future product. We'd get a percentage of the profits. Meanwhile we'd infiltrate the queer community. We were gathering information from all fronts to launch a perfect attack, to corner the market, to fill the Lord's coffers, and to clean up the city along the way. We needed Future's knowledge and facilities, Future needed a stronghold in the community and our funds, needed an innocent site for the clinic and

149

the computers which worked day and night scanning for data that Future could use."

It is as silent as fog coming in on little cat feet. Then the Computer Moll speaks. "And you found out about our network. Through me."

"What a gift from the Lord! Ole lived right upstairs from you. I'd tell him you were onto something big. It was nothing for him to learn to unlock a window from the fire escape and slip through. He could not lock it after him, but you were in the clouds, moping over that woman, and never noticed."

I look at Tallulah. "Ah-ha! So it is Big Ole who leaves the window open. Do I not tell you this means something?"

Tallulah licks a kiss onto her paw and blows it at me.

"Then," Mrs. Kling goes on, "he attaches the disk to a trained courier who delivers it to the computer center at the church," she says, eyeing the cats in the room.

"Where," Darlin' says, "you changed the data and transmitted, knowing you'd taken the guts out of the message."

"You've got it, you clever little fag." Mrs. Kling acts like she enjoys this show. Maybe she is like Rex, a blowhard show-off. "Then the cats returned the disks to Ole and went off to the lab to get their rewards. Future is a brilliant company. Using the cats kept everyone safer."

Dumpster growls with resentment. "So this is why Bad Tuna Gat sleeps on Big Ole's porch! To direct the operation!"

"Only partly," I say, feeling sad. "He is devoted

150

to Big Ole. Bad Tuna can never forgive himself for being on the side that kills Ole. It is a tragic case of profits before People."

The People go on talking. The Computer Moll says, "Ole would bring the disks back to Alice. But why did your cat hang around Alice when you visited?"

"We hoped if you noticed any changes you'd think it was the cat's magnetic collar. And this would tip us off that you were onto us when you banned the cat from your place."

Indeed, Rex is on his red cushion in the other room, kicking paper clips from his collar. The poodle is at his feet, chasing after then. Rex spits at him now and then.

"What about the other guys still at the clinic?" asks Darlin'.

"And," Tallulah whispers to me, "Yellow Ethel, the rest, are they going to die now?"

"I do not know," I answer. "Let us hope that if they receive 'cures' it prolongs their lives instead of cutting them short."

"I'll take care of 'the other guys' just like I'm taking care of you. And now that you know everything, you'll stay right where you are until my assistants polish them off and come for me. Enjoy your last moments while I call the doctor."

"Be serious," Ethan says.

This seems to enrage Mrs. Kling. She sets the phone back the hook. "I'll be serious, all right. I know what you did with my nephew when he thought he was dirt like you," she responds. She lunges for Ethan, the hypo headed straight for his heart.

151

Chapter 27

"The fatal cure, right, Mrs. Kling?" asks Darlin', boldly crossing to the couch. "The cure the doctor was about to give me? The opposite of what could make me well? Do you enjoy watching such horrible deaths?"

Darlin's words and movements attract her eyes and she hesitates just long enough to let Ethan twist out of reach.

Darlin' keeps up the yak. He grabs a big pillow from the couch and holds it in front of himself. He gets within spitting distance of her. "Is that what he did to the others? To my friends? Maybe they would have died anyway, maybe he could have cured them. Instead, they'd take a slow turn for the worse, wouldn't they, and twist and groan in agony until they died. But we're all just faggots, right? You don't mind killing off one, two, a dozen of us. Do you have enough in that hypo to infect me?" He moves in on her another step. "It's too late, Nurse Kling. I already have the disease. Inject me all you want, I'm already a living weapon. Isn't that what you say about persons with AIDS? Are you ready to pay for your fear of us?"

"Stay back," says Mrs. Kling with a swipe of the needle, her voice trembling. "Don't do anything you'll regret. The doctor will take care of you, boy. He can cure you. Just be nice to me."

Darlin' moves the pillow to deflect the attack. "And what about your beloved show cat, Nurse Kling? Are you leaving him behind? Surely you know you'll have to flee with all these new dead bodies at your feet."

Rex's ears stand up as tall as Coit Tower.

"That cat's a loser," says his People. "Like my sister. Like my sister, my nephew. Always bringing home stray kittens. As if I would want the dirty scraggly things. I told him I placed them through the church in nice homes. Half of them looked like his, the tomcat. As if I would've bothered. The last three I just dragged off to the clinic. Let them experiment on some young ones with this stuff," she says, stabbing toward Darlin' with the hype. "I would've taken Ole there too to get rid of him if he hadn't

153

threatened me. I could have. Then you wouldn't have traced all this to me and we could've finished our job before Judgment Day!"

Though I personally do not think this glacier can melt, she looks like she is about to cry.

Tallulah leans on me. "So that is where my kitnapped kittens go! And Rex thinks all along he is taking care of his kids when he turns them over to her!"

"Maybe he is not the complete welcher," I agree. I look toward him, but he is not on his cushion. He is in the air, hurtling toward his People whose back is turned while she menaces Darlin'. When he lands on the back of her neck Mrs. Kling's scream is louder than every siren in the city called out all at once. Rex hangs on.

Darlin' knocks the hypo to the floor. Levis grabs Rex and tosses him to us on the couch where he collapses, whimpering, hiding his face.

I hand the incriminating rhinestones to Dumpster. He leaps to the window and drops them out of sight. The Elders do not have to know Rex's part in all this.

Ethan is on the phone already, indeed calling out every siren in the city.

The Computer Moll races out to transmit the unaltered data to the world. Her earrings sound like a tambourine.

"Can you stand to comfort Rex?" I ask Tallulah.

She looks at him with compassion. "I can try."

"You are a courageous woman. I must do other work."

I signal for Dumpster and Turtle Dove to follow me outside.

"Quick, before the cops get here. I want you two to go over to the God Is Not Dead."

"What?" exclaims the Dump. "I do not set paw in there for a trillion dollars."

"How about for breakfast at Fisherman's Wharf?"

"Make it dinner."

"Deal," I agree. "I am cognizant of the fact that excess cat fur in the intestines of an electronic instrument such as a computer is not at all healthy for said machines."

Turtle Dove does an excited little dance. "I can tell you are Demetrius' sister!" she says. "You are brilliant too!"

Dumpster is thinking. "So you want us to get like affectionate with the computers and like lose as much stolen info as we can."

"Yes. Fur, claws, nail files, whatever weapons are handy."

"Emery boards?" asks Turtle Dove who commences to chatter about a sale on emery boards where she stacks up two hundred and fifty of the things for a mere pittance . . .

"Where do you go now?" asks Dumpster. "To collect the medal of honor?"

"No. To extricate the kittens from the doc's grip before he infects them. He doesn't know the grand experiment is over."

"Just a sec then," says Dumpster and dashes back inside where we see him jump into Levis's lap and rub against him. Then he returns.

"Thanks, Demetrius II. Thanks Turtle Dove," I say.

"Rain de toot," answers Dumpster. He takes off, but Turtle Dove hangs about.

155

I turn back to Levis. He stares in wonder at his lap where a roll of green takes the place of Dumpster.

"Money?" he is asking.

Darlin' stares too. "Certainly looks like money."

"Where did it come from? I'd swear it wasn't here before Sting jumped up. I don't get it. This is —" he counts. "Thousand dollar bills! Twenty of them!"

I look at Turtle Dove. She bats her lashes.

"Out of the sky!" crows Levis, looking at Darlin'. "This will go a long way to perfecting our cure."

I look at Turtle Dove.

"What can I tell you?" she asks. "Demetrius bribes Yellow Ethel to search the dead doc after you mention that Bad Tuna spills the beans regarding a slush fund. Sure enough, this is in the Doc's pocket."

She lifts her eyes to the windowsill where Dumpster departs. "That's my man."

Chapter 28

The welcome home shindig tossed by Turtle Dove for the lost kittens is something to see. Dove is related to this fancy-ass caterer over on Russian Hill and inveigles her to donate services and grub. How this is accomplished is simple: the caterer wishes to cash in on the publicity befalling Peacock Alley when the arrests are made and Future Pharmaceuticals and the God Is Not Dead church are shut down.

I do not know who has the in with San Francisco, but she puts on her prettiest sunshine for the occasion. Glenn Gull and friends do an aerial show to the music of Morty Mockingbird.

The All-Edison Orchestra is tuxedoed up and Woogie is at the piano on Tallulah's overhanging stage. Little Hot Paws, in a white satin marching suit with black shirt and white bow tie, wears five drums slung across her shoulders and over her back. Rat-a-tat, rat-a-tat, rat-a-tat, BOOM, she leads the parade up and down the Alley in which the found kittens cavort between phalanxes of Elders, Miss Kitty at the fore, Humphrey bringing up the rear like a snail rushing home. The stool pigeons line the route at the rooftops, cooing and ah-ing at the sight of us.

Rex cops a place of honor too, as father of the little lost kittens. Now that he lives with Ethan and Miss Kitty, he gives his rhinestone magnet collar to the poodle as a gesture of friendship. At his side is the mother of the kittens. She turns out to be Bad Tuna's younger sister, a kid more shy than the sun on a foggy day, no great looker, but who has it bad for Rex and is rumored to have more buns in the oven already.

Bad Tuna Gat, as the proud uncle, marches with his sidekick Roary. I am once of a mind to have him banned from the parade since he engineers the kitnapping, but he is family and my toots, Tallulah, claims he learns something from it all, especially around the incident of blowing the twenty thou. I can see on his face the toll Big Ole's death takes on him. There is guilt in every heavy step he takes, though he struts to hide it. When I confront him in regards to his deeds, he agrees to establish a kitty literature scholarship in the kittens' names.

Tailspin, one of the myriad cousins of the kittens who insist on their place in the sun, is duded up in tan vinyl. It is dollars to dog biscuits that he wears naugahyde shorts as an undergarment. Yellow Ethel is another cousin. The word is she leaves Leonora for someone her own age, gives the old heave-ho to the Feline Potential Movement and returns to school to study for a Private Eye degree.

Due to our considerable part in the denouement of the kitten affair, Tallulah, Dumpster, Turtle Dove and yours truly are requested to end the parade, which we do with all dignity. That is, which Tallulah and myself do with dignity. Dumpster limps behind with Humphrey not because of his three-leggedness, but due to the excess dinner to which I treat him as promised the previous night outside Fisherman's Wharf. Turtle Dove tosses riddles at the audience.

"How do you make an elephant float? Two scoops of ice cream, soda and an elephant!"

"How do you stop an elephant from charging? Take away his credit cards!"

"Why do elephants go to bed late? They spend hours setting their tails!"

Dolly Parrot shrieks with laughter from her window. She pitches feathers down instead of confetti.

Tallulah grins like a Cheshire cat. She repays me for exonerating her by marching at my side. I am of a mind to desire such a state to continue for a lifetime. She confides to me, in my arms last night, that she marches for her lost innocence as much as she marches for the kittens. Yet, she explains, she now achieves all she desires in life, and embraces me with passion.

We reach the stage. The tap dancing cats wait for

159

us. They lay formica flooring across the stage. Hot Paws climbs up. When everyone is still, Woogie strikes a chord. Hot Paws sets the beat. The Backstairs commence to dance.

As long as they do not dance all night on my ceiling, they are very good. Today they do a slow shuffle first, then faster, then so fast they whirl around the stage doing a number as shipshape and spazzed out and full of piss and vinegar as life. The audience roars for more, begins to dance in the aisles. The kittens are lifted to the stage, the copper-colored butterfly wings, the long brown stockings, and the copper-colored beret. Coached by the Backstairs, they do a little kitten jig, then get lost trying to run back to Rex and their mater.

Everykitty gets to rub their cheeks.

Tallulah looks at me. My whiskers are wet with tears.

"Despite your tough exterior, Big Girl, you are a pussy cat inside."

I straighten my suit and my fedora. "It is time for me to get back to the office, where I am needed."

Tallulah looks at me. "*I* need you, Big Girl, I need you."

"Ah, heck, Sweet Lips," I say, "want to come to Olley's with me, then? She has some snappy platters. Those Backstairs put me in a hoofing mood."

"Tell me, Sue Slate," asks Tallulah, in quite a sultry tone of voice, "does Olley have any slow tunes? Like 'An Affair To Remember'?"

In my heart it is the Fourth of July once more.

"Hey, Slate!" calls Turtle Dove.

"Uh-oh," says Tallulah Mimosa.

"Knock-knock!"

160

I roll my eyes, but determine to get this over with. "Who is there?"

"Cantaloupe."

"Cantaloupe who?"

"Cantaloupe with you tonight!"

Turtle Dove laughs all the way up the fire escape.

"That's a good one, Dove!" yells Dolly Parrot from above.

There is an abundance of laughter all around us when Tallulah asks me, "Cantaloupe?"

And yours truly, Sue Slate, Private Eye, answers, "Why not?"

A few of the publications of
THE NAIAD PRESS, INC.
P.O. Box 10543 ● Tallahassee, Florida 32302
Phone (904) 539-5965
Mail orders welcome. Please include 15% postage.

AFTER THE FIRE by Jane Rule. 256 pp. Warm, human novel
by this incomparable author. ISBN 0-941483-45-2 $8.95

SUE SLATE, PRIVATE EYE by Lee Lynch. 176 pp. The gay
folk of Peacock Alley are *all* cats. ISBN 0-941483-52-5   8.95

CHRIS by Randy Salem. 224 pp. Golden oldie. Handsome Chris
and her adventures. ISBN 0-941483-42-8   8.95

THREE WOMEN by Sally Singer. 232 pp. Golden oldie. A
triangle among wealthy sophisticates. ISBN 0-941483-43-6   8.95

RICE AND BEANS by Valeria Taylor. 232 pp. Love and
romance on poverty row. ISBN 0-941483-41-X   8.95

PLEASURES by Robbi Sommers. 204 pp. Unprecedented
eroticism. ISBN 0-941483-49-5   8.95

EDGEWISE by Camarin Grae. 372 pp. Spellbinding
adventure. ISBN 0-941483-19-3   9.95

FATAL REUNION by Claire McNab. 216 pp. 2nd Det. Inspec.
Carol Ashton mystery. ISBN 0-941483-40-1   8.95

KEEP TO ME STRANGER by Sarah Aldridge. 372 pp. Romance
set in a department store dynasty. ISBN 0-941483-38-X   9.95

HEARTSCAPE by Sue Gambill. 204 pp. American lesbian in
Portugal. ISBN 0-941483-33-9   8.95

IN THE BLOOD by Lauren Wright Douglas. 252 pp. Lesbian
science fiction adventure fantasy ISBN 0-941483-22-3   8.95

THE BEE'S KISS by Shirley Verel. 216 pp. Delicate, delicious
romance. ISBN 0-941483-36-3   8.95

RAGING MOTHER MOUNTAIN by Pat Emmerson. 264 pp.
Furosa Firechild's adventures in Wonderland. ISBN 0-941483-35-5   8.95

IN EVERY PORT by Karin Kallmaker. 228 pp. Jessica's sexy,
adventuresome travels. ISBN 0-941483-37-7   8.95

OF LOVE AND GLORY by Evelyn Kennedy. 192 pp. Exciting
WWII romance. ISBN 0-941483-32-0   8.95

CLICKING STONES by Nancy Tyler Glenn. 288 pp. Love
transcending time. ISBN 0-941483-31-2   8.95

SURVIVING SISTERS by Gail Pass. 252 pp. Powerful love
story. ISBN 0-941483-16-9   8.95

SOUTH OF THE LINE by Catherine Ennis. 216 pp. Civil War
adventure. ISBN 0-941483-29-0   8.95

WOMAN PLUS WOMAN by Dolores Klaich. 300 pp. Supurb
Lesbian overview.   ISBN 0-941483-28-2   9.95

SLOW DANCING AT MISS POLLY'S by Sheila Ortiz Taylor.
96 pp. Lesbian Poetry   ISBN 0-941483-30-4   7.95

DOUBLE DAUGHTER by Vicki P. McConnell. 216 pp. A Nyla
Wade Mystery, third in the series.   ISBN 0-941483-26-6   8.95

HEAVY GILT by Delores Klaich. 192 pp. Lesbian detective/
disappearing homophobes/upper class gay society.
                                           ISBN 0-941483-25-8   8.95

THE FINER GRAIN by Denise Ohio. 216 pp. Brilliant young
college lesbian novel.   ISBN 0-941483-11-8   8.95

THE AMAZON TRAIL by Lee Lynch. 216 pp. Life, travel & lore
of famous lesbian author.   ISBN 0-941483-27-4   8.95

HIGH CONTRAST by Jessie Lattimore. 264 pp. Women of the
Crystal Palace.   ISBN 0-941483-17-7   8.95

OCTOBER OBSESSION by Meredith More. Josie's rich, secret
Lesbian life.   ISBN 0-941483-18-5   8.95

LESBIAN CROSSROADS by Ruth Baetz. 276 pp. Contemporary
Lesbian lives.   ISBN 0-941483-21-5   9.95

BEFORE STONEWALL: THE MAKING OF A GAY AND
LESBIAN COMMUNITY by Andrea Weiss & Greta Schiller.
96 pp., 25 illus.   ISBN 0-941483-20-7   7.95

WE WALK THE BACK OF THE TIGER by Patricia A. Murphy.
192 pp. Romantic Lesbian novel/beginning women's movement.
                                           ISBN 0-941483-13-4   8.95

SUNDAY'S CHILD by Joyce Bright. 216 pp. Lesbian athletics, at
last the novel about sports.   ISBN 0-941483-12-6   8.95

OSTEN'S BAY by Zenobia N. Vole. 204 pp. Sizzling adventure
romance set on Bonaire.   ISBN 0-941483-15-0   8.95

LESSONS IN MURDER by Claire McNab. 216 pp. 1st Det. Inspec.
Carol Ashton mystery — erotic tension!.   ISBN 0-941483-14-2   8.95

YELLOWTHROAT by Penny Hayes. 240 pp. Margarita, bandit,
kidnaps Julia.   ISBN 0-941483-10-X   8.95

SAPPHISTRY: THE BOOK OF LESBIAN SEXUALITY by
Pat Califia. 3d edition, revised. 208 pp. ISBN 0-941483-24-X   8.95

CHERISHED LOVE by Evelyn Kennedy. 192 pp. Erotic
Lesbian love story.   ISBN 0-941483-08-8   8.95

LAST SEPTEMBER by Helen R. Hull. 208 pp. Six stories & a
glorious novella.   ISBN 0-941483-09-6   8.95

THE SECRET IN THE BIRD by Camarin Grae. 312 pp. Striking,
psychological suspense novel.   ISBN 0-941483-05-3   8.95

TO THE LIGHTNING by Catherine Ennis. 208 pp. Romantic
Lesbian 'Robinson Crusoe' adventure.　ISBN 0-941483-06-1　8.95

THE OTHER SIDE OF VENUS by Shirley Verel. 224 pp.
Luminous, romantic love story.　ISBN 0-941483-07-X　8.95

DREAMS AND SWORDS by Katherine V. Forrest. 192 pp.
Romantic, erotic, imaginative stories.　ISBN 0-941483-03-7　8.95

MEMORY BOARD by Jane Rule. 336 pp. Memorable novel
about an aging Lesbian couple.　ISBN 0-941483-02-9　8.95

THE ALWAYS ANONYMOUS BEAST by Lauren Wright
Douglas. 224 pp. A Caitlin Reese mystery. First in a series.
　ISBN 0-941483-04-5　8.95

SEARCHING FOR SPRING by Patricia A. Murphy. 224 pp.
Novel about the recovery of love.　ISBN 0-941483-00-2　8.95

DUSTY'S QUEEN OF HEARTS DINER by Lee Lynch. 240 pp.
Romantic blue-collar novel.　ISBN 0-941483-01-0　8.95

PARENTS MATTER by Ann Muller. 240 pp. Parents'
relationships with Lesbian daughters and gay sons.
　ISBN 0-930044-91-6　9.95

THE PEARLS by Shelley Smith. 176 pp. Passion and fun in
the Caribbean sun.　ISBN 0-930044-93-2　7.95

MAGDALENA by Sarah Aldridge. 352 pp. Epic Lesbian novel
set on three continents.　ISBN 0-930044-99-1　8.95

THE BLACK AND WHITE OF IT by Ann Allen Shockley.
144 pp. Short stories.　ISBN 0-930044-96-7　7.95

SAY JESUS AND COME TO ME by Ann Allen Shockley. 288
pp. Contemporary romance.　ISBN 0-930044-98-3　8.95

LOVING HER by Ann Allen Shockley. 192 pp. Romantic love
story.　ISBN 0-930044-97-5　7.95

MURDER AT THE NIGHTWOOD BAR by Katherine V.
Forrest. 240 pp. A Kate Delafield mystery. Second in a series.
　ISBN 0-930044-92-4　8.95

ZOE'S BOOK by Gail Pass. 224 pp. Passionate, obsessive love
story.　ISBN 0-930044-95-9　7.95

WINGED DANCER by Camarin Grae. 228 pp. Erotic Lesbian
adventure story.　ISBN 0-930044-88-6　8.95

PAZ by Camarin Grae. 336 pp. Romantic Lesbian adventurer
with the power to change the world.　ISBN 0-930044-89-4　8.95

SOUL SNATCHER by Camarin Grae. 224 pp. A puzzle, an
adventure, a mystery — Lesbian romance.　ISBN 0-930044-90-8　8.95

THE LOVE OF GOOD WOMEN by Isabel Miller. 224 pp.
Long-awaited new novel by the author of the beloved *Patience
and Sarah.*　ISBN 0-930044-81-9　8.95

WE TOO ARE DRIFTING by Gale Wilhelm. 128 pp. Timeless
Lesbian novel, a masterpiece. ISBN 0-930044-61-4   6.95

AMATEUR CITY by Katherine V. Forrest. 224 pp. A Kate
Delafield mystery. First in a series. ISBN 0-930044-55-X   7.95

THE SOPHIE HOROWITZ STORY by Sarah Schulman. 176
pp. Engaging novel of madcap intrigue. ISBN 0-930044-54-1   7.95

THE BURNTON WIDOWS by Vickie P. McConnell. 272 pp. A
Nyla Wade mystery, second in the series. ISBN 0-930044-52-5   7.95

OLD DYKE TALES by Lee Lynch. 224 pp. Extraordinary
stories of our diverse Lesbian lives. ISBN 0-930044-51-7   8.95

DAUGHTERS OF A CORAL DAWN by Katherine V. Forrest.
240 pp. Novel set in a Lesbian new world. ISBN 0-930044-50-9   7.95

THE PRICE OF SALT by Claire Morgan. 288 pp. A milestone
novel, a beloved classic. ISBN 0-930044-49-5   8.95

AGAINST THE SEASON by Jane Rule. 224 pp. Luminous,
complex novel of interrelationships. ISBN 0-930044-48-7   8.95

LOVERS IN THE PRESENT AFTERNOON by Kathleen
Fleming. 288 pp. A novel about recovery and growth.
ISBN 0-930044-46-0   8.95

TOOTHPICK HOUSE by Lee Lynch. 264 pp. Love between
two Lesbians of different classes. ISBN 0-930044-45-2   7.95

MADAME AURORA by Sarah Aldridge. 256 pp. Historical
novel featuring a charismatic "seer." ISBN 0-930044-44-4   7.95

CURIOUS WINE by Katherine V. Forrest. 176 pp. Passionate
Lesbian love story, a best-seller. ISBN 0-930044-43-6   8.95

BLACK LESBIAN IN WHITE AMERICA by Anita Cornwell.
141 pp. Stories, essays, autobiography. ISBN 0-930044-41-X   7.50

CONTRACT WITH THE WORLD by Jane Rule. 340 pp.
Powerful, panoramic novel of gay life. ISBN 0-930044-28-2   7.95

MRS. PORTER'S LETTER by Vicki P. McConnell. 224 pp.
The first Nyla Wade mystery. ISBN 0-930044-29-0   7.95

TO THE CLEVELAND STATION by Carol Anne Douglas.
192 pp. Interracial Lesbian love story. ISBN 0-930044-27-4   6.95

THE NESTING PLACE by Sarah Aldridge. 224 pp. A
three-woman triangle—love conquers all! ISBN 0-930044-26-6   7.95

THIS IS NOT FOR YOU by Jane Rule. 284 pp. A letter to a
beloved is also an intricate novel. ISBN 0-930044-25-8   8.95

FAULTLINE by Sheila Ortiz Taylor. 140 pp. Warm, funny,
literate story of a startling family. ISBN 0-930044-24-X   6.95

THE LESBIAN IN LITERATURE by Barbara Grier. 3d ed.
Foreword by Maida Tilchen. 240 pp. Comprehensive bibliography.
Literary ratings; rare photos. ISBN 0-930044-23-1   7.95

ANNA'S COUNTRY by Elizabeth Lang. 208 pp. A woman
finds her Lesbian identity.   ISBN 0-930044-19-3   6.95

PRISM by Valerie Taylor. 158 pp. A love affair between two
women in their sixties.   ISBN 0-930044-18-5   6.95

BLACK LESBIANS: AN ANNOTATED BIBLIOGRAPHY
compiled by J. R. Roberts. Foreword by Barbara Smith. 112 pp.
Award-winning bibliography.   ISBN 0-930044-21-5   5.95

THE MARQUISE AND THE NOVICE by Victoria Ramstetter.
108 pp. A Lesbian Gothic novel.   ISBN 0-930044-16-9   6.95

OUTLANDER by Jane Rule. 207 pp. Short stories and essays
by one of our finest writers.   ISBN 0-930044-17-7   8.95

ALL TRUE LOVERS by Sarah Aldridge. 292 pp. Romantic
novel set in the 1930s and 1940s.   ISBN 0-930044-10-X   7.95

A WOMAN APPEARED TO ME by Renee Vivien. 65 pp. A
classic; translated by Jeannette H. Foster.   ISBN 0-930044-06-1   5.00

CYTHEREA'S BREATH by Sarah Aldridge. 240 pp. Romantic
novel about women's entrance into medicine.
                                               ISBN 0-930044-02-9   6.95

TOTTIE by Sarah Aldridge. 181 pp. Lesbian romance in the
turmoil of the sixties.   ISBN 0-930044-01-0   6.95

THE LATECOMER by Sarah Aldridge. 107 pp. A delicate love
story.   ISBN 0-930044-00-2   6.95

ODD GIRL OUT by Ann Bannon.   ISBN 0-930044-83-5   5.95

I AM A WOMAN by Ann Bannon.   ISBN 0-930044-84-3   5.95

WOMEN IN THE SHADOWS by Ann Bannon.
                                               ISBN 0-930044-85-1   5.95

JOURNEY TO A WOMAN by Ann Bannon.
                                               ISBN 0-930044-86-X   5.95

BEEBO BRINKER by Ann Bannon.   ISBN 0-930044-87-8   5.95
        Legendary novels written in the fifties and sixties,
              set in the gay mecca of Greenwich Village.

VOLUTE BOOKS

JOURNEY TO FULFILLMENT   Early classics by Valerie   3.95

A WORLD WITHOUT MEN   Taylor: The Erika Frohmann   3.95

RETURN TO LESBOS   series.   3.95

These are just a few of the many Naiad Press titles — we are the oldest and
largest lesbian/feminist publishing company in the world. Please request a
complete catalog. We offer personal service; we encourage and welcome
direct mail orders from individuals who have limited access to bookstores
carrying our publications.